CHERISH THE DREAM

Darcie Westbrook is determined not to let herself be hurt by another man, but she can't help falling for vet Glenn Hunter who is a regular visitor at her animal sanctuary. A property developer is out to take her land and build a housing estate on it, and someone is attacking horses. It is only when Glenn's life is in danger, as he fights to protect the horses, that Darcie admits her true feelings for him.

TERESA ASHBY

CHERISH THE DREAM

Complete and Unabridged

LINFORD
Leicester

First published in Great Britain in 1995

First Linford Edition
published 2012

British Library CIP Data

Ashby, Teresa.
    Cherish the dream. - -
    (Linford romance library)
    1. Love stories.
    2. Large type books.
    I. Title II. Series
    823.9'2–dc23

    ISBN 978–1–4448–0962–6

Published by
F. A. Thorpe (Publishing)
Anstey, Leicestershire

Set by Words & Graphics Ltd.
Anstey, Leicestershire
Printed and bound in Great Britain by
T. J. International Ltd., Padstow, Cornwall

This book is printed on acid-free paper

1

The early-morning sun was rising in the east, staining the gathering clouds a watery red. It was an ominous warning of coming storms. The slight breeze was gathering in strength, promising to become an icy wind.

Glenn Hunter had been crouching on the hill beside the pet-carrier since the cold, pre-dawn period. He'd expected to be finished here by the time the sun came up, but it was proving to be a forlorn expectation.

'Come on,' he said softly. 'If you leave it much longer, I'll have to take you back to the surgery! I've got other patients to see, you know.'

At last a dark nose appeared at the open door. Glenn held his breath, afraid that if he made a sound, the animal would retreat back into the carrier. Whiskers twitched, then a pair of bright, golden eyes looked up at him.

The young fox had been found lying injured at the side of the road. It had been hit by a car, but was not as badly hurt as it had first appeared.

Glenn treated the fox's cuts and grazes, and now it was fully recovered it was time for it to return to the wild.

The trouble was, it seemed reluctant to leave.

Glenn waited, then suddenly it shot out of the carrier and raced off down the hill towards a blackthorn hedge without so much as a backward glance of thanks for it's release.

There's gratitude for you, Glenn thought, smiling to himself.

'Glenn!'

He turned abruptly and saw Joe Nelson, senior partner of Nelson and Partners, Veterinary Practice, striding towards him.

'Ah, Glenn, there you are. We were supposed to have breakfast at eight with Darcie Westbrook,' Joe reminded him.

'She wasn't best pleased when you didn't turn up!'

'I'm sorry, Joe. I lost all track of time,' Glenn said, closing up the carrier and lifting it off the ground. 'I didn't expect releasing the fox back into the wild would take this long. I thought he'd have been off like a shot.'

'It's surprising just how frightened a wild thing can be. Talking of wild things, don't apologise to me.' Joe chuckled. 'It's Darcie you should be saying sorry to. She's hopping mad! It's not a good start here for you, Glenn.'

The two men walked up the slope together to where Joe's estate car was parked behind Glenn's Land-Rover.

'I don't think she's forgiven you yet for last time,' Joe remarked as they stopped beside Glenn's car. 'And believe me, Darcie can be one of the most unforgiving of women! I should know. She used to work for me.'

'I had a good excuse for not turning up at her little tea party,' the younger vet said defensively. 'I was up at Fenn

Farm with Lord Horrington's favourite horse!'

'Oh, dear,' Joe said, still chuckling as if he found the whole situation highly amusing. 'For two people who've never met, you've certainly become a thorny subject with each other!'

'Maybe I'll call in later after morning surgery,' Glenn said thoughtfully. 'I haven't time to do it now.'

'I'd do that if I were you,' Joe said approvingly. 'It's not that she's particularly touchy about keeping appointments, but she can't afford to waste food — and she'd cooked us up a wonderful breakfast!' He rubbed his stomach in satisfaction. 'You missed a treat there, Glenn.'

'Hmm,' Glenn murmured. 'Seems all I'll be getting to eat today is humble pie and lots of it!'

'Looks like a storm's brewing,' Joe remarked, nodding towards the blood red sky. 'October's an unpredictable month. A bit like our Darcie really,' he added with a mischievous glint in his eyes. 'One minute she's raging like a gale, the next she's as calm and sweet as sunshine after the rain.'

Darcie Westbrook, legend in her own lifetime, Glenn thought as he drove the Land-Rover down the rutted track leading back to the main road. He'd heard all about her from various sources. To some she was a saint, to others nothing short of a pain in the neck!

Eccentric, kind, crazy, sweet, there was no end to the words he'd heard used to describe her. Well, she was bossy! He'd reached that conclusion all on his own. There was never an invitation to call, but a summons, an order. *You will come for breakfast on the eighteenth*! The 'or else' was unspoken, but there all the same.

She ran an animal sanctuary from a big, but rundown, Victorian, one-time vicarage. He passed it on the way back to the surgery, a rambling, ivy-covered place with crumbling brickwork and peeling paint. He slowed down as he passed, but saw no sign of the legendary Darcie Westbrook — not that he had any particular wish to.

As he speeded up again, he wondered about Horrington's very own female St Francis. While people were apt to give him enthusiastic descriptions of her character and personality, no-one ever told him what she looked like. He had a picture of her in his mind though, a very clear idea of how she looked. A woman in her mid-fifties with a bush of grey hair she never had time to have cut. She'd speak with a booming voice, never listen to a word anyone else had to say and terrify the life out of anyone of a nervous disposition!

★ ★ ★

How could anyone sleep through all that racket, Glenn wondered as he looked down at the girl sprawled out and sound asleep on the concrete at the back of the kennels.

She was leaning against the wall, her

head on one side, resting on her shoulder. He sighed and looked around.

Surely someone had heard him ring the bell? If not, then they must wonder why the place was in uproar. It seemed that every one of the eighteen dogs in residence was barking or howling — or both!

He looked back at the girl. She must be one of the students from the college who occasionally came in to lend a hand.

Her legs, clad in ripped jeans, were out straight and across them lay a large black cat. It looked up at Glenn and yawned, displaying a mouthful of sharp, white teeth and a healthy pink tongue.

There was nothing else for it. Loath as he was to disturb her, he'd have to wake the girl up. He reached out his hand and the cat began to growl.

He ignored it and shook her by the shoulder. It was his first mistake, the first of many he was to reflect afterwards. The cat hissed a warning a split second before it raked its claws across the back of his hand.

'Ow!' he cried. The skin rose before his eyes, the scratch going white before pin pricks of blood appeared along its length.

Instinctively, he put his hand to his mouth. Incredibly, the girl was still fast asleep, undisturbed by the cat's rapid movements.

'Hello,' he said, not wanting to risk touching her again. The cat was still growling, deep and low in its throat. 'Excuse me, miss!'

Her long, golden hair was tied back in a loose pony-tail. A strand fell across her face as she stirred.

'Oh, ow!' she groaned, rubbing her neck.

He crouched down in front of her and grinned as she opened her eyes.

'What beautiful eyes you have,' he said, forgetting for a moment about his injured hand.

The compliment wasn't intended as empty flattery. She really did have gorgeous eyes, the kind he'd like to lose himself in. Dark, deep pools in her soft, pale face.

As he gazed into them, he noticed little golden flecks sparking in the brown as she looked startled, then cross.

'Who are you?' she demanded. 'Who let you in?'

The cat, put out by the sudden anger in her voice when he had been enjoying a peaceful nap, leaped up and ran off to sit a few feet away, furiously licking his tail.

'I let myself in,' he explained. 'I rang the bell and as no-one answered, I thought — '

'That you'd come snooping!' she finished for him, an angry light coming into her eyes.

Glenn straightened up and offered her his hand. She pointedly ignored it as she got to her feet.

'Ow!' she cried again.

Glenn watched bemused as she hopped from one foot to the other.

'Pins and needles,' she explained. 'I'll

be all right in a minute. Don't worry.'

'I'm not.' He grinned, enjoying the spectacle. Her hair finally escaped the band and cascaded down around her shoulders like a silken curtain.

She stopped leaping about, grabbed a handful of her hair and wound the band tightly around it. The end result was a lop-sided pony-tail.

'I'd get it chopped off if I had the time,' she muttered furiously.

'That would be a shame.' He smiled and, judging by the cross look on her face, his remark seemed to irritate her. 'You have lovely hair.'

'Who are you?'

'Glenn Hunter.' He offered his hand and this time she took it. She had a surprisingly firm grip for someone so small. He winced with pain and she turned his hand and looked at the angry weal.

'How did you do that?'

'He did it.' He pointed accusingly at the cat who was still preening. 'Savage beast.'

'He probably thought you were going to attack me. He's very suspicious of strangers,' she said, eyeing him speculatively. 'And extremely protective. What are you doing here?'

'I'm looking for Darcie Westbrook.'

She withdrew her hand and immediately speculation turned to out-and-out suspicion. The cat had nothing on her when it came to dishing out dirty looks.

'What do you want her for?'

'Just a quick word,' he said. 'Is she around?'

'She might be.'

'Are you always so helpful?'

'We'd better do something about that hand,' she said, looking again at the scratch. 'I've got some antiseptic somewhere. I take it you are up to date with your tetanus jabs?'

He laughed. He would have told her that, being a vet, of course he was, but she didn't give him the chance.

'There's nothing funny about tetanus,' she said grumpily. 'You'd better come with me.'

She led the way into a small room, part of the annexe to the main house. The annexe was L-shaped and housed the kennels, the cattery and an office and reception area.

'I know I've got a first aid kit here somewhere,' she muttered as she rummaged through an untidy stationery cupboard. 'Ah, here it is. Sit down.'

He sat down on a stool while she diluted some antiseptic liquid in a stainless steel bowl. Without preamble, she grabbed his hand and dabbed the scratch with cotton wool. He winced, but whatever she might think, it wasn't caused by pain. When she took his hand in hers, he'd felt his heartbeat quicken, his pulses race.

No, it wasn't pain troubling him, but something far more pleasant. It was worth getting scratched if it meant he'd get this much attention from such a lovely woman.

'Don't be such a baby,' she said briskly as she cut off a strip of plaster and stuck it to the back of his hand.

'It's only a scratch. There you are.'

Her tone implied that she'd finished with him.

'About Darcie Westbrook . . . ' he began.

'Have you a donation for her?'

'No — '

'Are you here to offer an animal a loving home?'

'No — '

'Then she's not available,' she said as she pushed the first aid kit back into the cupboard. 'Now if you'll excuse me, I have a lot to do.'

She turned away from him, picking up a blue, metal tool-box and walked out of the office and away down the side of the building. As she strode off, the cat trotted along at her heels like a graceful black shadow.

'Miss . . . ' Glenn called after her, but she was obviously in a great hurry.

He didn't know what it was about her, but something had hooked him. Maybe it was the way her shiny pony-tail swung from side to side, or the way his skin had tingled when she touched his hand. Whatever it was, he only knew that he wanted to get to know her better.

His mouth felt dry. He swallowed hard and followed her round the corner where he found her standing in front of a partially-built shed, the tool-box now at her feet.

'The new cattery,' she said, sensing him behind her.

'I get it.' Glenn risked hazarding a guess. 'You're a carpenter!'

'Stone cold,' she responded, keeping her back to him.

Even though she was cross, she had a very quiet voice, but it was deep and resonant. What a fascinating woman, he thought to himself. He was definitely going to enjoy living in Horrington!

'Look, Miss — ' he said.

She turned slowly to look up at him and he was aware again of her eyes. They were dark brown, almost the same colour as mahogany, and slightly slanted. He'd completely forgotten about Darcie Westbrook! All he knew was that he wanted to get to know this particular young lady a lot better.

'What is it you want, Mr . . . ' She frowned as she struggled to remember his name. He felt hurt that she'd forgotten so quickly.

'Hunter,' he said. 'Glenn Hunter, and you are . . . ?'

'Very busy,' she said, looking at her arm where a white band of skin encircled her wrist. 'I'll tell Darcie you were here.'

Suddenly realisation struck him. This was Darcie Westbrook — this young, beautiful, fiery woman. He caught her hand and held it within his own for a moment. Their eyes met and there was a tangible clash, felt but unseen. It knocked the breath out of Glenn and tinged Darcie's cheeks pink.

'Where's your watch?'

She snatched her hand away. For the first time since he'd woken her, she looked uncomfortable.

'I lost it.'

15

'I heard Darcie Westbrook sold her watch to raise funds,' he said. 'It was the last thing she owned of any value and belonged to her late grandmother. It was worth a lot of money — '

'All right, so now you know,' she said. 'I'm Darcie Westbrook. So if you're here to serve a writ on me, get on with it. If not, please go away.'

'A writ?'

She laughed softly.

'I thought not, but unless you're offering a home to one of the animals, I haven't time to talk to you. I want to get the felt on to this roof before we get any more rainfall.'

'On your own?'

'Do you see anyone else here?' She gestured with her hands.

'Then I'll help,' he said.

She stared at him for a moment as if she was weighing him up.

'You don't look as if you've come from the council,' she said at last. 'And I don't imagine you picked up that tan sitting in an office.'

He looked down at himself and wished he'd made the effort to clean up before coming here. He was wearing jeans with mud spatters around the bottoms and a blue-check, padded shirt. The whole ensemble sported a generous coating of animal fur.

'Will I do?' He laughed, letting her know he was aware of her appraisal. She had a wide, generous mouth, but her expression was giving nothing away. She still looked suspicious, reminding him of the fox he'd released earlier. It had never quite trusted him either.

'Who are you?'

'I told you.' He grinned. 'Glenn Hunter.'

'What are you?' she demanded.

'That's why I'm here,' he said. 'To introduce myself. I thought Joe Nelson told you about me.'

Her eyes widened and she slapped her own forehead.

'Glenn Hunter,' she cried. 'The new vet!'

'That's me.'

'You're a little late, Mr Hunter,' she remarked coldly. 'Breakfast was over hours ago. I fed yours to the dogs.'

'I really am sorry,' he said quickly, aware that he was very nearly grovelling.

'Do you make a habit of standing people up, Mr Hunter? You embarrassed Joe and you inconvenienced me. And it wasn't the first time either!'

'I'm aware of that,' he said, his blue eyes twinkling. He was beginning to wish he'd turned up earlier — and not because she was cross with him. 'Won't you just accept my apology?'

'Accepted,' she said with a smile, her anger just a pretence. 'Joe explained about the fox. Did you release it on Furze Hill?'

'Yes, why?'

'It's council-owned land. The hunt's been banned from it, so at least he should be safe, so long as he stays within its boundaries.'

'I had a word with him before he left,' Glenn told her seriously. 'I gave him the full lecture about keeping off the roads and not fraternising with hounds!'

She gave him what he could only describe as a cautious smile.

'I had a vixen here once. It took a long while to gain her trust, but once I had . . . They're such gentle animals. They don't deserve all the bad Press they get.'

'I won't argue with that.'

She was about to say something, when a bell jarred loudly.

'Excuse me, Mr Hunter,' she said and hurried off towards reception.

Glenn looked up at the shed when she'd gone. If she'd done it alone, then she'd done well, he thought. The roof felt was held in place by house bricks, waiting to be tacked into place.

He still felt he ought to make amends for missing breakfast this morning. What was it his dear old granny used to say? 'Actions speak louder than words.'

2

When Darcie came back an hour later, Glenn was kneeling on the roof tapping nails through the felt. She stood watching him for a moment, hands on hips.

'I hope you're knocking those nails in straight,' she called. 'I can't bear shoddy workmanship.'

The nerve of the girl! He was doing her a favour out of the goodness of his heart, and she had the bare-faced cheek to imply that he wasn't up to it!

He was about to come back with a sharp retort when he realised she was smiling. What a difference it made to her face.

'I've made some coffee,' she said. 'I think you've earned it. I'm sorry I left you alone so long. I half expected you to have gone.'

He climbed down from the roof and

wiped his hands on his jeans. He stood beside Darcie and they both looked up at the shed.

'I'm hoping this will be our salvation,' she said quietly. 'I'm often asked if I'll take boarders. When people go away on holiday, they like to know their pets are being looked after properly. I intend to open for boarders just before the Christmas holiday.'

'There's no fortune to be made in boarding kennels,' Glenn remarked. 'Will you go in for quarantine as well?'

'No,' she said emphatically. 'Too much red tape. My life's complicated enough as it is. Once I get the roof sorted out, I'll get some wire and finish the runs. It's important for animals to be able to lie in the sun, wouldn't you agree, Mr Hunter?'

'It's Glenn,' he said. 'Didn't you say something about coffee?'

'Sorry, yes, it's in the house, Mr Glenn.'

She walked off and he watched her go, rubbing his head in puzzlement.

Had she been joking when she said that? He ran to catch up with her.

'Glenn,' he repeated. 'That's my name. Glenn Hunter.'

'Double barrelled?'

'You Darcie, me Glenn!' He laughed.

'Oh, sorry.' She flushed and laughed, too. 'I must seem very dense to you. I'm just tired. That's why I crashed out in the yard. I seemed to spend all last night looking for Bess, our resident basset-hound. She got her nose down to the ground yesterday afternoon and went off. You know how bassets are! No matter how much I called, she completely ignored me. Usually, I manage to catch up with her, but last night, she gave me the slip. I finally found her just after four this morning, sniffing and snorting in the churchyard! I just sat down for five minutes to gather my thoughts and give Puss a cuddle, and the next I knew, you were shaking me awake.'

He stepped into the house behind her. An ancient Jack Russell was asleep curled up on top of a stool, more cats were sprawled about, but it was the black one she'd called Puss that ran over to her.

He yowled a greeting which sounded very much like, 'Hello!' and wrapped himself round her legs.

'I'm not surprised you're exhausted,' he remarked. 'Eighteen dogs and goodness knows how many cats must keep you on the go all day. Joe says you give each of them a run every day.'

'That's right.' She smiled. 'And there are seventeen dogs now. That was Heidi Williams from The Wheatsheaf at the door. Her Labrador, Harold, died last week — '

'I put him down,' Glenn said. 'Had to. The poor old chap's kidneys had failed. She said she wouldn't get another.'

'I had a youthful, chocolate Lab in the kennels,' she said. 'Heidi couldn't resist him. She won't forget Harold, but Nugget will keep her so busy she won't have time to mope. Sit down.'

'How do you cope, Darcie?' Glenn asked.

'I'm not on my own all the time,' she said. 'Students come in from the college now and then to give me a hand. They're a good bunch of kids. I can't pay them and goodness knows, they could use the extra money, but still they come.'

Glenn sat and almost at once, Puss leaped on to his lap and began to purr loudly.

'Oh, friends now are we?' Glenn laughed and tickled Puss's head.

The cat responded by flinging himself over on to his back, offering his tummy for tickling. Glenn obliged, cradling the cat in the crook of his arm like a baby.

'You're honoured indeed,' Darcie remarked with a smile. 'Puss doesn't take to just anyone. He's normally an extremely good judge of character.'

'Normally?' Glenn queried. 'How about you?'

'Oh, I like to take a little longer to

make up my mind about someone,' she replied enigmatically.

Her eyes were dancing. Did she feel it, too, he wondered, this magnetic, irresistible attraction he felt for her? He hoped so, with all his heart he hoped so . . .

'So you'll be taking over from Joe when he retires next spring,' she said, shaking him out of his reverie.

While his thoughts had been wandering unleashed along romantic avenues, hers had been on the straight path of business. He felt ridiculously disappointed.

'That's right,' he said quickly. 'Starting next week I'll be dropping in to see you every day. Joe will call now and then, but he's hoping to gradually wind down his work load.'

'Yes, he explained all that this morning.'

'I'm sorry, am I keeping you?' he said, aware that she was suddenly distracted.

'No, I . . . ' She paused, listened. 'I

thought I heard a car pull up . . . '

The bell rang three times and she jumped to her feet. Puss anticipated Glenn's next move and jumped to the floor.

'What is it?'

She looked frightened.

'There's only one person I know who rings the bell like that,' she muttered. 'Excuse me.'

★　★　★

The dogs were all barking again. Glenn followed her out of the house towards the annexe. It was time he was leaving anyway.

If it was someone else coming to give a home to a dog, he'd slip out quietly. Not saying goodbye would give him an excuse to come back!

'I thought I told you not to come here again,' he heard Darcie saying and he paused just outside the reception area.

'And I told you I'd not done with you, Miss Westbrook!'

'I'll call the police — '

'Call them! The law's on my side, or will be once I convince the local council to act.'

'It won't get your anywhere,' Darcie retorted. 'I run this place by the book. They can't shut me down without good reason.'

'Maybe a good reason's all they're waiting for.'

Glenn stepped out suddenly behind Darcie. The man responsible for harassing her was stocky, in his mid-forties. He was wearing a crumpled suit and when he saw Glenn his mouth dropped open.

'Perhaps you should introduce me to your friend, Darcie,' Glen suggested.

'He's no friend of mine,' Darcie muttered. 'Gifford Harvey, the builder — '

Before she could introduce him, Glenn said, 'Ah, the Greenfields estate.'

'You know it?'

'Of course,' Glenn replied with an air of casual indifference. 'How could I miss it?'

How could anyone miss the estate? It

looked like a scar on the landscape, an out of place mish-mash of grey and red roofs. Gifford Harvey had crammed as many houses as possible into a small area and the end result was as unattractive as it was alien.

'It's a prime location,' Gifford Harvey said, puffing himself up. 'People are moving away from London in their droves. They want country life within commuting distance of London and Suffolk is ideal.'

But Horrington, with its ancient, sixteenth-century buildings and a church dating back to Norman times, was in danger of losing something very special.

'Mr Harvey wants my land, including this house for use as part of a new estate,' Darcie explained. 'And we're both after Eighty Acres. I want to be able to rehouse horses and goats and — well, anything that needs some space.'

'And I want to build homes for people! I happen to think people are more important than animals, Miss Westbrook!'

Eighty Acres was a sprawl of land including ten acres of woodland adjoining Darcie's property. It even had a large pond.

'This house is a ruin.' Gifford Harvey held up his hands. 'It wants tearing down — '

'So you can build more of your little boxes?' Darcie cried. 'No, Mr Harvey. This house has been in my family for generations. I won't see it torn down to make room for more of your featureless properties.'

'It's not just the land and the house.' Gifford Harvey ignored Darcie and addressed himself to Glenn now, man to man, cutting Darcie out completely. 'It's the noise and the smell. If I go ahead and buy and develop Eighty Acres, this place will put would-be buyers off.'

'What utter nonsense,' Darcie snapped. 'No-one living on your estate could possibly hear the dogs — and they don't smell!'

'What about the youths that come

here? They terrorise the local residents, going round in gangs.'

'There's never more than half a dozen and they're perfectly decent, young people.' Darcie leaped to the defence of her army of helpers.

'Then there's the health hazard. There's that disease children get from dog's muck . . . '

'Unnecessary if the animal is regularly wormed.' Glenn spoke with quiet authority. 'Which Miss Westbrook's animals are.'

'You only have her word for that,' Gifford Harvey cried triumphantly. 'Mark my words, miss, I'll have this place closed down one way or another. I'd advise you to take the money I'm offering you and run, because once you have to go, the offer will go down.'

Darcie was about to speak, but Glenn placed his hand gently on her arm.

'Is that a threat, Mr Harvey?' he asked.

'I'm just stating the truth,' Gifford Harvey said. 'I've got friends on the council who want to see this place shut down as much as I do.'

'Ah, corruption,' Glenn said knowingly.

'You're twisting my words!'

'Am I? Perhaps you'd better leave, Mr Harvey.'

'You haven't heard the last of me, miss.' Gifford Harvey waved his finger in Darcie's face. 'I'll be back — '

'I understand Miss Westbrook told you not to come here again,' Glenn said. 'Will it take a court order and all the adverse publicity that goes with it to make you comply with her wishes?'

Gifford Harvey turned on his heel and stormed out, slamming the door behind him.

'Good thing I was here,' Glenn said. 'Are you all right, Darcie?'

She was shaking, whether with fear or anger, he couldn't be sure. She turned slowly to look at him and he deduced from the look on her face, that it was anger. It came as an even greater surprise to realise it was directed at him.

'How dare you?'

'What . . . ?'

'I don't need anyone to fight my battles for me, do you understand? Who do you think you are? What are you doing threatening to get court orders? I can't afford to go to court over this. I'm on my own, Glenn Hunter. I don't need anyone else.'

'You can't let him come here and threaten you like that,' Glenn reasoned. 'It's not on, Darcie.'

He reached out and placed his hands squarely on her shoulders.

'And you're not on your own.'

She looked up at him. Her hair had started another escape bid and had fallen over her face. He brushed it back and saw tears shimmering in her eyes. Maybe she wasn't as tough as she was making out, or maybe the pressure was finally getting to her.

Under the circumstances there was only one thing he could do. It was what he'd wanted to do from the very first moment she'd opened her beautiful eyes and looked at him. He pulled her gently into his arms and held her face against his chest, stroking her hair as if she were a child.

Then he made his next big mistake. He kissed the top of her head.

She jumped away from him like a scalded cat, hugging her arms around herself, staring at him with a mixture of fear and hostility in her eyes.

'Darcie, I . . . ' He reached out, but she flinched away from him. His bewilderment turned to fury. She was behaving as if he'd tried to attacked her, when all he'd done was to kiss the top of her head!

'Go away,' she whispered. 'Please, just go away.'

There was something about her voice, the way it caught, that made her sound vulnerable. It made his sudden anger dissolve.

'I have to go away. I'm due in surgery. Goodbye, Darcie, and thanks for the coffee.'

As he strode away, he knew she was crying, but he also knew that if he returned and tried to comfort her, she'd probably scratch his eyes out. Just like that damned unpredictable blow hot and cold cat of hers!

★   ★   ★

Puss sat on Darcie's lap, pushing his face up hard under her chin, knocking her head back. He'd dribbled down the front of her shirt and was purring loud enough to drown out the radio.

'Hey, easy,' she said, laughing as she tickled his ears. 'I know what you're after!' She broke off a piece of her toast for him.

'As I thought,' she murmured as he jumped off her lap and down on to the floor with his prize. 'Cupboard love!'

The old Jack Russell — named Jack by the traffic police who had brought him in — hopped down from his stool and stood looking from Puss to Darcie, his expression most accusing. Puss growled a warning.

'That's enough of that,' Darcie said, pretending to be cross. 'Jack won't steal your toast, Puss. Here, Jack. Sit.'

The small, plump terrier sat and lifted his paw and the remains of Darcie's breakfast quickly disappeared. With a sigh, she got up and took her dishes to the sink. She'd already fed all the animals and given them fresh drinking water.

Rejects, one and all, she thought sadly. And that includes me. A sudden wave of self pity washed over her, but she fought it back before it could get a hold. She'd been there, down that slippery slope where only darkness and misery lay in wait . . .

Suddenly Puss ran out of the kitchen, low to the ground, growling angrily.

'What is it, Puss?'

Jack licked his lips, looked hopefully for more toast, then realising he'd had his lot, retired to his perch on the stool. Goodness knew how old he was. He'd seemed ancient, almost on his last legs when he'd been found wandering around beside a dual carriageway — and that was six years ago.

And really, for Darcie, it had all started then. Jack had been the first, then came Puss and one by one, the others until commonsense told her she'd have to give up work and devote her life to these animals.

Commonsense, she asked herself harshly, or circumstances?

The bell jarred, Jack gave a small token woof and Darcie hurried off to answer it . . .

'It was making a funny noise, so I brought it along to you. You don't mind, do you, Darcie?'

'You did the right thing, Betty,' Darcie said, smiling at the old lady.

'I would have taken it to the vet, but it's a long walk and I can't walk as far as I used to. Besides, you're an animal nurse, so I thought you'd know what to do.'

In the old days, Betty would have been branded a witch and ostracised by the community. She lived alone in a tiny cottage at the edge of the wood, her only companion an ancient, stiff-legged, black mongrel called Mandy.

Darcie turned her attention to the sack Betty had carried in and placed on the table. The same table on which yesterday, Glenn Hunter had rested his arm while she bathed it. The thought was a fleeting, but disturbing one. Darcie returned her attention to the sack.

Obviously an animal was imprisoned inside, but Betty was too nervous to open the bag up herself, so she'd put it in an old push chair and pushed it all the way to the sanctuary.

Darcie took a penknife from her jeans pocket and sliced through the rope.

'Where did you say you found it?'

'Under the bridge,' Betty said, her rheumy eyes wide. 'The water had washed it up against the river. I was just taking Mandy for her early-morning walk when I saw it.'

Darcie hesitated for just a moment

before opening the sack, afraid of what she'd find. Carefully, she pulled it open. Inside, sodden and bedraggled, was a tabby cat. She was thin, shivering, her ribs sticking through her fur, but as soon as she saw Darcie, she let out a heart-wrenching yowl that said she was very much alive!

'Poor darling,' Darcie murmured softly. 'It's all right. You're safe now.'

'Careful . . . ' Betty warned as Darcie reached out to lift the cat. 'Cats can be vicious animals.'

'She's just terrified.' Darcie was careful to keep her voice soft and even so she didn't frighten or startle the animal. 'I won't hurt you. Pass me that towel, would you, Betty, please?'

Her tone was soothing and gentle. The cat's ears were flattened against her head, but as Darcie spoke, the ears rose slightly in response. Gently, Darcie patted the soaked fur, sponging out the water.

'Good girl. I'm not going to hurt you.'

At first, Darcie stroked the cat with slow, gentle movements until she felt the tension in the animal begin to recede.

'There now . . . '

As she lifted the cat into her arms, wrapping it in the towel Betty had passed to her, Betty said, 'It's purring.' Her voice was tinged with disbelief as she added. 'Who'd have thought . . . '

'Sometimes purring can be an indication of great pain and discomfort in a cat. But I don't think that's the case here. She's beautiful, Betty.'

Darcie looked again into the bag and her heart gave a painful lurch.

'Poor little things,' Betty muttered crossly. 'Who'd do such a dreadful thing? They ought to be strung up!'

Darcie quite agreed. Her heart was thudding painfully and for a moment, she was just too angry and choked to speak, then . . .

'Hold on,' she cried. 'I'm sure I saw movement. Here — hold her while I have a closer look.'

Betty, reluctantly, took the mother cat into her arms while Darcie lifted the kittens from the sack one at a time. She examined each in turn.

There was absolutely no doubt that the three smaller ones were dead, but the biggest, a ginger one, was breathing shallowly.

'I'll call Joe Nelson,' Darcie said. She placed the kitten inside her jumper. It felt frozen and wet against her skin, but it desperately needed warmth.

Her heart filled with hope that life might yet spring from that disgusting sack. She tried not to think of the other three, how they must have suffered . . .

3

'Where's Joe?' Darcie said as soon as Glenn strode into the warm kitchen. He was the last person she wanted to see right now. She was still feeling unsettled from their last meeting.

His eyes, as cold and blue as a January sky, glared at her and she realised her greeting had been less than welcoming.

'Busy,' he retorted, a little tightly. 'Won't I do?'

'Of course,' she said breathlessly. She didn't like Glenn Hunter, didn't like the peculiar effect he had on her or the way his eyes lingered whenever he looked into her eyes.

Darcie liked to be in control, and when Glenn was around, she wasn't. Far from it. I've been let down too badly, once too often by good-looking men and should know better, she thought crossly. Anyway, the way he's looking at me right now, I've probably put him off for life!

'I'll look at the mother first,' Glenn said.

Darcie watched as he checked the cat over. He spoke soothingly as his big hands probed gently, his firm, careful fingers pressing the cat's abdomen.

'She's very thin,' he said at last, glancing at Darcie as he spoke. 'But you don't need me to tell you that. She's almost certainly riddled with worms and who knows what else.'

She felt a strange jolt. Was his angry look intended for her, or for the people who had dumped the cat and her kittens in the river? She put it down to his male pride. She must have wounded his when she told him to keep out of her life. Well, that was his problem, not hers.

'What do you think?' she asked, and cursed her voice for coming out shaky.

'She'll be fine,' he said. 'She needs a lot of building up and plenty of tender, loving care, but she's young — I'd say no more than a year old.'

He turned to Darcie. He was grinning now. The sudden change in his expression took her by surprise.

'Is that a kitten in your sweater?' he asked.

'I've been keeping him warm.'

'Best place for him,' Glenn said, still grinning. 'OK, let's have a look. Gently does it.'

Darcie carefully brought out the kitten. Almost immediately it began to shiver and mewed pathetically.

'Warm in there, was it?' Glenn said, taking the tiny creature in his huge hands. His voice was gentle, soft and it touched something deep inside Darcie she'd thought long dead.

Darcie watched closely as Glenn checked the kitten over. His grin had gone to be replaced with a more grave expression. His frown was so deep that his dark eyebrows almost touched in the middle.

That's a sign of a bad temper, she

thought. Beneath that easy-going, happy-go-lucky exterior there's an ogre lurking.

He looked up and saw Darcie and Betty watching him like a pair of hawks.

'I don't hold out much hope,' he said softly.

'I do,' Darcie said. 'He survived the river and the cold. He's a fighter, Glenn. He deserves every chance.'

'Why do I get the feeling that if I don't do something to save the kitten's life, I'll never leave this place alive?'

Darcie glared at him. Joe Nelson said Glenn Hunter was a good, young vet, one of the best. She couldn't believe he'd give up on the kitten that easily. He met her gaze steadily for a moment, then sighed.

'I said I didn't hold out much hope. I didn't say I wouldn't try. Warmth and nourishment.' He looked straight at Darcie, his expression darkly sombre. 'Same as for the mother. I'm going to give them both a shot to boost them up, give them a kick start if you like. I don't want to raise your hopes. He could still

44

die. But care is going to be very time consuming, Darcie. The kitten will have to be bottle fed. There's no way he'll get anything from his mother.'

'No problem,' she said. 'I've done it before.'

'It's a lot of work for anyone,' he argued. 'You're already pushing yourself to the limits. And do you think Puss is going to tolerate another male around the place?'

'Who says I'll keep him?' she demanded, already knowing in her heart she would.

'I do. There's no way you can give this animal the love and attention he needs then hand him over to someone else. I know you only too well already, Darcie Westbrook.'

'I've bottle fed litters before!' She tossed back her hair. She felt disconcerted that he imagined he knew her already. No-one got that close to her any more, no-one. Only she knew the real Darcie Westbrook.

'Litters,' he said slowly. 'This is one

animal. One to one. You'll form a very close bond. Darcie, listen to me, you can't do it.'

'I did it with Puss! He's been with me since he was three weeks old!'

'I rest my case!'

Betty's eyes darted from one to the other as if she were watching a tennis match. When they fell silent, she heaved an impatient sigh as if eager for them to continue.

'Betty . . . ?' Darcie turned to her.

'Oh, no.' Betty threw up her hands. 'No way! No cats. I don't even like cats. Besides, my old dog wouldn't stand for it. Mandy hates cats and it wouldn't be right to upset her at her age.'

'All right then, Mr Hunter, what's your solution — other than putting him down?'

Glenn lifted up the kitten. It looked lost in the palm of one of his big hands. Hands that were huge, but gentle with fingers that were very long and tapered, almost artistic.

Now he was dry, the kitten's fur was

golden and fluffy and his slate-blue eyes quite bright.

He'll live, Darcie decided. He's got that look about him. He wants to live.

'Well, Mr Hunter?'

'Easy,' he said, 'I'll take him.'

'You will! But how? I mean, you're a vet, how will you ever find the time?'

'Why not?' He turned the kitten round, looking at it from all angles. It looked back at him and yawned, bringing a smile to Glenn's face and a painful tug at Darcie's heart. 'He'll get the best possible care with me.'

'He'd get the best possible care with me!' Darcie countered, her smile vanishing. She could feel herself bristling. If she were a cat, her hackles would be up. How dare this outsider turn up and insinuate that she wasn't capable of nursing a kitten?

'Do you have to take everything as a personal insult?'

Betty's eyes started bouncing back and forth in their sockets again. A little smile tipped the corners of her mouth.

'Do you have to keep assuming that I'm incapable of managing things?'

Glenn's eyebrows knotted again. He looked exasperated.

'You know, you're the strangest woman I've ever met! You won't accept help, you distrust everyone you meet. What is it with you?'

'Maybe you've just never met anyone like me before,' she retorted.

If she hadn't been so angry, she would have smiled. She couldn't remember the last time she'd argued like this! It made a change from arguing with people about their treatment of animals! Or with Gifford Harvey!

'That's true,' he said with a look of pure exasperation. 'I'm sure I would have remembered if I had!'

He opened his bag and prepared syringes for the cats.

'As soon as she's strong enough, I'll spay her,' he said of the mother cat, then he saw Darcie and Betty exchange knowing smiles and went on, 'Well, I can't keep her kitten and not her! She'll be able to help me nurse him back to health.'

'She's just a baby herself,' Darcie said, cuddling the cat close. 'She needs lots of love and care, too.'

He stroked her and gently caught up the skin at the back of her neck while Darcie held her. 'She's so thin,' he said disgustedly as he injected her. 'I'd love to get my hands on whoever did this.'

'So would I,' Darcie muttered.

'Then we do agree on something.'

He was grinning and despite herself, Darcie smiled, too. She'd never met anyone with such vivid blue eyes before.

'There,' he said, gently rubbing the cat's neck. 'All done. I'll take her home with me and start her with light meals, little and often. I doubt her poor stomach is used to getting much at a time.'

He picked up the kitten. 'As for this little fellow,' he said. 'I dare say he'll eat like a hungry bear once he picks up.'

'You will . . . ' she began.

'I will take care of him, I promise,' he said, his voice gently reassuring. 'They'll both have the best of care. I'll take him everywhere with me and during surgery hours, I'll leave him in the office so I can nip in and feed him between patients.'

'What about nights?'

'I've got an alarm clock,' he said. 'It's very reliable. It's called a telephone and it's guaranteed to wake me at regular intervals.'

With that, he placed the kitten and its mother inside his jacket and picked up his bag.

'Come along, Betty. I'll give you a lift home.'

'But it's out of your way,' Betty protested.

'I'm going that way,' he said, winking at Darcie. 'You would like a ride home, wouldn't you?'

'Well, yes, so long as it won't be any trouble.'

He rolled his eyes and held the door open for her.

'Mr Hunter — Glenn,' Darcie said. 'Breakfast, tomorrow — seven o'clock.'

★ ★ ★

Glenn gave Betty a helping hand into the Land-Rover. Once she was in the seat, she looked quite pleased with herself.

'It's high, isn't it?' she said.

'Can you manage the seat-belt, or . . .'

'You can do it for me, dear,' she said. 'I can't get my fingers round those things.'

He could feel the cats inside his jacket, warm and cosy against his chest. I must be crazy, he thought. He'd been planning to get a dog to ease the loneliness and quiet of Hill House — but a cat! Two cats if the mother made up her mind to stay.

Hill House was a rambling, old place, smothered in ivy and perched, as the name suggested, at the top of a hill. The garden was huge and overgrown and

Glenn sometimes wished he'd bought something smaller, less draughty.

He didn't really feel at home there and was looking for a decent-sized piece of land on which to build his own house.

He transferred the cat and kitten to a carrier in the back of the car, wrapping them round with a soft blanket. They snuggled up close together, the mother cat drawing her rough pink tongue across her kitten's head, and he felt his throat go dry as anger began to rise again.

Shaking it off, he got into the car beside Betty and grinned.

'Breakfast with Darcie,' he mused aloud as they drove off.

'She only invites favoured people to breakfast,' Betty said. 'Otherwise, if she doesn't like them — she eats them for breakfast!'

Betty burst out laughing, cackling like an old crone until she had Glenn laughing, too.

'I wouldn't like to get on her wrong

side,' he remarked.

'Aw, it's not the girl's fault she's the way she is,' Betty said, then stopped, leaving Glenn hanging in mid air.

'Go on,' he said at length. 'You can't tell me half a story!'

'It's not for me to say,' she said, clasping her hands together in her lap. 'I don't like gossip. Still, it isn't gossip really, not as such.'

He eased off the accelerator, not wanting to get to Betty's house too quickly. He already knew there was more to Darcie Westbrook than met the eye and he wanted to know all of it.

'Would you mind popping in to see Mandy?' she said abruptly, frustratingly changing the subject. 'She's got a sore on her leg. Right raw it is and she keeps on at it, chewing and licking . . . Sometimes, it bleeds.'

'Of course,' he said.

'I'll make you a cup of tea. Just don't let Mandy see the cats. She hates cats.'

'I'll leave them in the back. They'll be

warm enough, while I come in and see Mandy.'

He turned into the rutted, muddy lane that led down to Betty's cottage and pulled up on the grassy verge out front. This would have been more up my street, he thought. Cosy little place, couple of rooms, nice and private.

He changed his mind when she led him inside. He had to stoop to get through the door. Living somewhere like this, he'd either have a permanent headache — or a stiff neck!

The old, black dog was a little deaf and didn't hear them come in. Once she realised, she gave a token bark and hobbled stiffly to greet them. She sniffed curiously at Glenn's hand.

Mandy had the beauty of age. Her face was white and her gait stiff, but she had that gentle look that came with passing years.

Glenn warmed to her at once, more so when she licked his hand. If only all his patients were as friendly, he thought. Then again, any of his patients who weren't friendly usually had good reason not to be.

'Hello, old girl,' he said, kneeling down. He could see at once what Betty was worried about. On one of her hind legs was a raw patch about the size of a ten pence piece.

Mandy growled softly and stiffened when he touched it.

'All right, Mandy,' he said. 'You don't mean that, sweetheart. I know it's sore.'

'Is it — is it cancer?' Betty stammered.

'No, Betty,' he said, straightening up and smiling down at her. 'It's what we call a lick sore. Basically, it starts as an itchy spot. She licks it, nibbles it and irritates the nerve endings, which makes it itch more and so it goes on until it becomes a vicious cycle. Eventually, once the fur is licked away, an ulcer forms. I'll give her some antibiotics for the infection and an injection to stop the irritation. If she keeps worrying it, I'm afraid it might have to be a bucket-on-the-head job!'

Betty looked relieved that it wasn't anything too serious, but there was still a look of uncertainty in her eyes.

'Betty, what's wrong?'

'Will it . . . ' She took a deep breath and straightened up. He could see she was struggling with her pride. 'Will it cost much?'

Once the question was asked, it seemed to give her the courage to go on.

'I don't begrudge spending money on her, but — but I just don't have very much and — and I'd have to pay you a bit every week — '

Betty was a proud woman and Glenn knew she wouldn't accept charity. He thought quickly, searching for a solution she would accept.

'There'll be no charge, Betty. Call it payment for rescuing the cat and her kitten. You walked all that way to Darcie Westbrook's place and I know that couldn't have been easy for you. You've a good heart, Betty. If only there were more people like you.'

Betty's face lit up.

'I'll make that tea I promised you. Will you have a scone, too?'

★ ★ ★

Sitting in Betty's kitchen with the morning sun streaming in a dappled beam through the trees, Glenn raised the subject of Darcie's past again.

'Poor girl,' Betty said. 'We all thought David was wrong for her, but he was rich, handsome and she was head over heels in love with him. Her parents and sister had flown all the way from Australia and her grandmother had hired a marquee for the reception and the whole village was invited to come along and join in with the celebration.'

Betty sighed and looked thoughtful for a moment, then she remembered the tea and poured it into two cups.

'And . . . ' he prompted.

'It was the middle of July. A beautiful summer day with not a cloud in the sky. Our little church was packed. I'd been all day the day before doing the flowers. We all wanted to make it special for Darcie, you see.

'Her parents emigrated when she was sixteen, but Darcie just refused to go and leave her grandmother. They had a very special relationship. It must have torn her in half having to make that decision, but the whole village had taken her to their hearts.'

Betty sighed and rested her hands in her lap, staring at her gnarled fingers for a few moments.

'She'd always been popular here though. Her father was a G.P. He was a good man, but he never made any secret of his disappointment when she refused to follow in his footsteps. She was such a plucky little thing to stand up to him the way she did.'

Betty fell silent, remembering, then, realising she was straying from the subject, started to speak again. 'Anyway — I'll never forget. She arrived at the church in a horse-drawn carriage — just like a princess. Her father was sitting beside her, looking so proud and handsome, but our Darcie . . . She looked so lovely . . . Everyone had come to see her married — everyone.'

Betty broke off and dabbed the tears from her eyes.

'He didn't turn up, you see. She laughed at first and said she'd better go for a trot round the block, but after a while, nobody was laughing. He'd jilted her. And in front of everyone!'

'Good grief,' Glenn whispered. 'The poor girl. How humiliating.'

'It changed her, of course it did,' Betty went on. 'Made her bitter. The best thing would have been for her to go away, back to Australia with her parents, but that's not Darcie's way.

'She's never run from trouble in her life and then of course, there was her grandmother. She wouldn't have left her. About a year on, her grandmother died, leaving the house to her and that's when Darcie started her animal sanctuary. She had several waifs by then anyway. That was two years ago. She used to be such a happy child, nothing ever fazed her, until that brute . . . '

Glenn was shocked to see more tears shimmering in Betty's eyes. If someone who had simply witnessed Darcie's humiliation still felt so strongly, how on earth must the poor girl feel herself?

'Call me a silly, old woman,' she said almost venomously, 'but a young girl's heart should never be broken so cruelly. I know that broken hearts are all part and parcel of life, but the way it was done, that's what really gets to me. There was no need to do that to her.'

'She's not had a lot of luck,' Glenn remarked.

'Luck doesn't come into it. And don't go pitying her. She'll hate that,' Betty said. 'For all she's been through, Darcie's never lost her compassion. And the girl's got her pride. If she thinks for one minute that you feel sorry for her, that'll be it!'

'Sorry for her!' Glenn laughed. 'I'm scared stiff of the woman!'

Betty's eyes twinkled. 'I know that's

not true,' she said. 'All I'm saying . . . The reason I'm telling you all this . . . ' She broke off and sighed. 'Please just promise me, Mr Hunter — Glenn — promise me you won't hurt her.'

'I'd never do that,' he said and found himself adding an afterthought, if only I could get close enough!

He looked up at Betty and found her staring at him, as if she could read his thoughts. She was smiling and nodding slowly.

'I believe you,' she said.

Still, he thought. Better to play things cool from now on. No wonder he'd got her back up with the way he'd been behaving. Typical Taurean, like a bull at a gate. Well not any more, he decided firmly. From now on, their relationship would be strictly business — at least until he'd won her trust.

4

'Well done,' Darcie said, smiling happily. 'You're bang on time! How's the kitten?'

It was nice to see her smile for a change, Glenn thought. She either looked so damned defensive or just so downright scared, she had him terrified of saying or doing the wrong thing!

He walked into the kitchen and sat down at the table, opening his jacket a little so the kitten peeked out.

'Oh!' Darcie cried, her delight obvious and genuine. 'He's looking fitter already!'

'Being clean and dry and having a full stomach helps,' Glenn said. 'As for his mum, she's found a sunny spot in the conservatory and won't budge! Now she's been cleaned, you'd be surprised what a beauty she is.'

'I doubt it,' she said. 'I've seen how

the most bedraggled-looking creature can turn into something of immense beauty, just by being clean and happy.'

His mouth began to water when she placed a huge plate of bacon, eggs and sausages in front of him.

'What have I done to deserve all this?' he said. 'I normally only have a slice of toast!'

Darcie sat down and he noticed she only had a slice of toast spread with marmalade.

'Where's yours?' he said suspiciously. He knew she was hard up and had the awful feeling he was eating her out of house and home!

To his amazement, she began to giggle, then laugh.

'Did I cut myself shaving?' he said, pressing his fingers to his face. 'What? Have I left one of my curlers in?'

She laughed even more.

'I'm sorry,' she said at last. 'It isn't you — it's me. I'm not very good at subtlety. Mr Vaughan, from the farm shop, keeps bringing me bags of food.

You see, everyone in Horrington seems to think I need looking after — and feeding up. I haven't the heart to tell Mr Vaughan that I don't eat meat any more.'

'So you didn't invite me here out of the goodness of your heart,' he said, his disappointment only partly a pretence. 'But because you wanted to get rid of your excess bacon!'

'I'm sorry, it's not just that. I thought it would be nice to get to know each other a bit better. We're going to be working together quite a lot over the next few years and it would be easier if we were friends.'

'Sounds good to me,' he said and began to eat.

Darcie watched him clear his plate. There was nothing wrong in liking a man, she told herself. It wasn't written down anywhere that she had to fall in love with him. After all, she got along fine with most of the men in the village.

'Can I warm this?' Glenn produced a bottle of milk from his pocket. 'It's time for Plato's breakfast.'

'Plato?' She took the bottle and stood it in a jug of hot water.

'Like it? I thought it was a bit more unusual than Tigger, Ginger or Garfield! Most of my marmalade clients have those names already.'

'What about his mother?'

'I haven't thought of a name for her yet.'

'How about Thetis. That's Greek, too.'

'Thetis, yes, I like that. Ah, perhaps I should have called the kitten Achilles, as he was Thetis's son,' Glenn pondered. 'No, doesn't suit him. I'll stick with Plato.'

They both laughed. Darcie reached out and stroked the kitten. Little as he was, he began to purr noisily.

'He's actually getting a little milk from his mother. Who knows, I may be able to let her take over once she's strong enough.'

She took the bottle from the jug, tested some of the milk on the inside of her wrist, then dried the bottle and handed it to Glenn.

Watching as he gave Plato the bottle, Darcie felt anger start to rise inside her like a tidal wave as once again the thought came, how could anyone be so cruel . . .

'Don't,' Glenn said softly, as if he knew exactly how she was feeling. 'It's done. You could torment yourself to death thinking about it.'

She nodded and blinked back tears of frustration and anger. 'You're right,' she said. 'More coffee, Glenn?'

'Does someone give that to you, too?'

'No, I buy the coffee,' she replied. 'Sometimes I think it's all that keeps me awake.'

'If you go on like this, you're going to burn yourself out,' he remarked. 'You look all in already and it's only just breakfast time.'

Darcie was so furious, she couldn't speak. All in! Had he any idea of the effort she'd gone to this morning? Getting up half an hour early so she could wash her hair and dab on a little make-up — making herself look half presentable and for what? Just to be told she was burned-out!

Well, thank you very much, Glenn Hunter, master of tact, that's the last time I make any sort of effort for you! Not that she'd made the effort for him, she told herself firmly, not in the least. She'd done it for herself, to revive her flagging spirits. Glenn Hunter had nothing whatsoever to do with it.

The kitten had a strong suck and was slurping at the bottle, dribbling excess milk down the front of Glenn's shirt. It was the only sound following Glenn's last statement. The air was heavy as Darcie's expression became stony.

'This is my life, Glenn. The last thing I need right now is someone like you telling me how to run it.'

'Perhaps you do,' he countered. 'Perhaps that's exactly what you need. There's no-one to tell you to slow down.'

'I don't need looking after, Mr Hunter!' Darcie cried, getting up from the table and going over to the sink. She started clattering dishes in the washing up bowl. 'I'm perfectly capable of taking care of myself. I don't need anyone else and I certainly don't need you lecturing me!'

'OK, Darcie.' He was on his feet and beside her in an instant. 'We're agreed on that. You don't need anyone else in your life, but when you collapse from exhaustion, who will take care of your animals? Had you thought of that? You're not a machine, Darcie.'

'I think you'd better leave now, Glenn,' she murmured softly. 'I've a lot to get through today.'

He stepped back and sighed deeply. 'I'll help you wash up.'

'I don't . . . '

'I know!' He threw his hands up in despair. 'I know. You don't need any help. Well, fine, I'll go then.'

He scooped up the kitten and tucked him inside his jacket.

'Come on, Plato. We've got work to do.'

Darcie waited until she heard his car drive away before growling, 'What a stupid name for a cat! What a stupid man. I hate Glenn Hunter. How I wish I'd never set eyes on him.'

But a well of despair was rising inside her. He was right. She knew that. She was dead on her feet and no amount of make-up could conceal the dark rings beneath her eyes. And in her heart she knew she wouldn't be able to cope on her own much longer.

Then what?

She shook her head miserably. It didn't bear thinking about . . .

'Ssh!' Darcie hissed. 'It's the men from the council. Look — they're surveying Eighty Acres.'

Darcie knew without looking around that it was Glenn coming up behind her. She knew the sound of his car, the way he gunned the engine before switching off the ignition, the way he rang the bell before entering.

She even knew the faint tangy smell of his cologne.

He'd been calling in every day for a week now and she'd always contrived to be rushed off her feet.

'They'll be deciding whether to grant Harvey permission to build his boxes, or whether the area should remain as it is — which it would if I had it!'

She glanced over her shoulder and felt the odd leaping of her heart that she'd somehow come to expect whenever he put in an appearance. I'll get over it, she told herself. Nothing to worry about!

'Why are we whispering?' Glenn asked. 'They can't possibly hear us from here!'

Darcie straightened up. 'The council have been slapping preservation orders on trees right, left and centre! They won't let Harvey ruin that land, will they?'

'Let's hope not. I thought you were broke, Darcie. How are you going to afford to buy that land?'

'I'm broke, but the sanctuary isn't. My grandmother had a collection of dolls and teddy bears. She used to exhibit them. They're worth a small fortune. She left them for the sole purpose of funding the sanctuary.'

'You'd sell them?'

'They're just toys, Glenn.'

She turned away from the fence and walked briskly towards the kennel block. He strode along behind her, quickly catching up and falling into step at her side.

'They sound in good form!'

'Waiting for their morning run,' Darcie replied. 'I'd like you to look at the Dane while you're here.'

'Bernie? Sure. What's wrong?'

'He's been vomiting. I've put him in the isolation kennel, but ... ' She shrugged, looking worried.

★　★　★

The news was not good. When he'd completed his examination of the Dane, Glenn straightened up.

'He's going to need an operation.'

She nodded. 'Do what ever you have to, Glenn.'

'I'll need a nurse. Karen's off sick and Ruth Nelson has gone to Bury St Edmunds.' He looked at her questioningly.

'I'll come with you.'

'What about this place?'

Distractedly she waved her hand. 'Philip's here. One of my helpers. I — I'll just go and tell him what's happening with Bernie . . . '

Darcie tried to make herself forget it was Bernie lying on the operating table as she watched Glenn work. She had to. It was a matter of self preservation, for the minute she started to think of him as Bernie, she risked falling apart.

'Can you do anything?'

'No,' he answered shortly. 'It's going to be kinder to let him go. I won't bring him round from the anaesthetic.'

For a while, there was silence in the surgery as Glenn neatly stitched the incision he'd made in the abdomen, taking as much care as if the dog would be up and running around again in a few days. Darcie bit down hard on her lip, trying to stop herself from bursting into tears. Her throat ached with the effort.

'That's it. He's gone.' Glenn's voice was harsh as he turned to look at Darcie. He turned away and drove his fist against the wall. 'Damn it!'

Darcie flinched. She could understand his anger, his frustration, she felt it herself.

'You did all you could.' Her words sounded so empty, so feeble and useless.

She couldn't take her eyes off Bernie. He'd always been so trusting, such a lovable, great lump. And as gentle as a lamb with any other creature, whether it was a kitten or a child.

Reaching out, she stroked the great head. He hadn't an angry bone in his body. Bernie had loved everyone and everything, even Puss. It was hard to imagine not looking out of the kitchen window and seeing him padding around in the big exercise pen.

Glenn turned back to face her, his eyes glittering. 'Yes, I did all I could. I could never have excised the tumour and even if I had, his life wouldn't have been worth living. Who wants an incontinent, crippled dog? You couldn't have nursed him, Darcie — and neither could I.'

The door opened and Joe Nelson walked in.

'What's all this? I could hear you outside, Glenn.' He walked over to the operating table and looked down at the dog. 'Is that Bernie?'

Briefly Glenn explained what had happened. Joe took a closer look at the dog and nodded.

'You let him go?'

'Yes,' Glenn answered shortly.

Joe put a hand on each of their shoulders and drew them close to him. He sighed deeply.

'Bernie was one hell of a dog,' he said. 'A great character. He liked nothing better than loping round the field with the other dogs. A happy dog, yes, that's how I think of Bernie, and that's how you must remember him.'

Darcie drew in her breath and almost sobbed. She knew she mustn't think of the dog on the table as dear old Bernie. It was just another patient. She must remember that.

'Now, just supposing that you successfully removed all traces of the tumour. I don't think he would have thanked you, either of you, for saving his life.'

'It was so quick,' Darcie spoke at last, her voice shaky. 'This time yesterday he was fine . . .'

It was no use. She couldn't control her grief. It came at her in a violent rush, making the room spin. Joe was speaking, but his voice sounded muffled and distant.

'Take her outside, Glenn. I'll finish off in here. Go on, be quick about it, before she faints or something!'

'I won't faint!' Darcie protested. 'I'm not the fainting . . .'

5

Darcie tried to sit up, but Glenn pushed her gently back down. Looking around, she recognised Joe Nelson's sitting room, the chintz curtains, the paintings of horses on the walls. Turning to the door, she saw Ruth Nelson coming in with a tray.

'Joe told me what happened.' She set the tray down on the broad oak coffee table. 'I thought you could both do with a cup of tea. I'm sorry about Bernie, really I am. He was a super dog.'

'Thanks, Ruth.' Glenn took a cup from Ruth and handed it to Darcie. 'Need any help?'

She struggled to sit up, rejecting his offer of help, and demanded, 'What happened?'

'You, em — you fainted,' Glenn said with an almost apologetic smile.

'I don't faint! I've never fainted in my life!'

She saw the looks Ruth and Glenn exchanged and her cheeks burned with embarrassment. How could she let herself down like that in front of Glenn Hunter of all people! He must think she was a real sap!

'I'll leave you to it,' Ruth whispered. 'I promised I'd help Joe in surgery.'

'I'll do it,' Glenn volunteered. 'You look all in, Ruth. You haven't caught 'flu off Karen, have you?'

'Probably.' She shrugged her shoulders ruefully.

The phone started to ring. Glenn gave Ruth's shoulder a squeeze before hurrying off to answer it.

'He's a good lad,' she told Darcie as soon as he was out of earshot. 'But he cares too much. Joe used to be like that. Many's the time I'd wake up in the middle of the night and find him sitting by the window, gazing out at the stars.'

'Joe? But he's so — so laid back now. He takes everything in his stride, even death and cruelty.'

'Oh, don't let that fool you. He still feels it here.' She clenched her fist and held it against her breast. 'But he can cope with it these days. He weighs up the good against the bad and the good always comes out on top. He sends more people and pets home happy and healthy than not.'

Darcie sipped her tea. It was hot and sweet and very welcome.

'Darcie, dear — have you heard from your parents lately?'

'Mum writes me a long letter once a month.'

'You're not sorry you didn't go with them, then?'

Darcie considered for a moment, then shook her head. 'I wouldn't have missed the last few years I spent with Nan for anything. Anyway, my home is here. I like Australia when I went out there for a visit, but . . .'

She broke off, realising there was something praying on Ruth's mind.

'Why do you ask, Ruth?'

The older woman looked at her and, with an apologetic shrug, said, 'You see, I was wondering about writing to your parents.' She licked her lips nervously. 'I'm worried about you, Darcie. And when I got back from Bury and saw Glenn carrying you in here — '

'Glenn carried me?'

'How else do you suppose they got you from the surgery? It's not like you to pass out, Darcie, and you look so tired, dear.'

The door clattered open and Glenn burst in.

'Sorry,' he said. 'Darcie, I need you. Are you feeling fit?'

'Yes, I — what?'

She put her cup down with a clatter and swung her legs down. Fighting back a brief wave of dizziness, she got to her feet.

'What is it, Glenn?' Ruth clasped her hands together, her pale green eyes filled with concern.

'Rookery Farm,' he said. 'Apparently old George Cooper has collapsed.

Goodness knows how long he's been lying there, but all his animals are in desperate need of attention.'

'And George?' Ruth asked.

'They've taken him to hospital. Looks as if he may have had a stroke. I'm sorry, Ruth. You'll have to help Joe after all. Ready, Darcie?'

★ ★ ★

'Thank goodness George doesn't pump them full of hormones to increase their milk production,' Glenn remarked as he felt a cow's bulging udder. 'Any good at milking, Darcie?'

She nodded. George's farm was very small. He kept just two cows, a small herd of goats and a few chickens. Everything he produced was organic and his proud boast was, 'These youngsters think they invented organic food, but I've never produced anything else!'

'Good girl. It's not as bad as I feared. I'll leave you to it while I take a look at the goats.'

'Thanks a bunch.' Darcie grinned wryly. 'Do you want me to collect the eggs and box them when I've finished?' she added, jokingly.

'Good idea. I'll give you a hand with that,' he said perfectly seriously. 'George's hens lay their eggs all over the place!'

She watched him stride off across the field, then turned her attention to the cows. Her heart softened as they looked pleadingly at her, their huge, gentle eyes filled with trust.

'All right lasses,' she said. 'Step into the byre.'

There was no place for milking machines at Rookery Farm and as Darcie found a stool, the cows hurried into their stalls, impatient to be relieved of their burden of milk. She tipped a little feed out for them and they munched contentedly while she milked them.

It was something she'd learned to do as a small girl — right here, at Rookery Farm as a matter of fact. Her father had been called out to one of George's daughters, Jeannie, who had tonsillitis and while he was busy, George had taken Darcie to the barn.

Her father had been horrified.

'Go and wash your hands at once, Darcie!' he'd snapped on her return, ignoring the fact that she was mightily pleased with herself. 'You've dirt all over your dress. What will your mother say?'

Quite frankly, Darcie didn't care. It had felt so nice, resting her head up against the warm side of the cow and seeing the bucket filling up as she gently, but firmly manipulated the teat.

When she'd finished in the byre, she went out into the golden sunshine and looked for Glenn. He was gathering eggs.

'I bet you never thought you'd end up doing that when you were at veterinary college!' She laughed at his startled expression.

'I call this public relations.' He grinned. 'Being a vet in a small place like this isn't just about looking after animals. It's about fixing roofs and . . . '

He broke off, his eyes twinkling dangerously. Darcie's heart flipped. Oh, how she liked him. He was nothing like David, nothing at all. In a million years, she couldn't see David possessing the same understanding as Glenn.

'How were the goats?' she asked.

'Fine.

'Darcie, we've got company.'

A car was trundling down the rutted lane towards the house.

'It's Jeannie!' Darcie cried. 'George's daughter.'

She ran across the grass, reaching the front of the house just as the car stopped. A young woman with cropped, dyed-red hair jumped out and embraced Darcie. She was wearing brilliant, multi-coloured leggings and a lime-green shirt. She looked, Darcie thought, absolutely dazzling. There was no other word for her.

'How are you? You look wonderful!' Darcie cried, holding her old school friend at arms length so she could have a good look at her. 'It's been so long, Jeannie.'

'I'm fine,' Jeannie said, frowning. 'But you're looking thinner, Darcie. Haven't you gotten over that rat yet? Oh, who's this? I say, Darcie! Where did you find him?'

'He's not mine!' Colour flared in Darcie's normally pale face as she hissed a denial. 'I can't stand the man!'

Glenn strode up, smiling handsomely as he held out his hand towards Jeannie. Darcie felt a prickle of unease. Had he heard her aside to Jeannie? She hadn't really mean it to come out like that, in fact, she hadn't really mean it at all. It was just her stupid, clumsy way of keeping up appearances.

Quickly, she regained her composure and got on with the introductions.

'Jeannie, this is Glenn Hunter. He's Joe Nelson's new partner. Glenn, this is Jeannie Cooper, George's daughter.'

Her voice was tight as she spoke and she felt her lips clamp together as

Jeannie and Glenn exchanged greetings that seemed to her to be just a little too friendly.

'Have you been to the hospital?' she asked, reminding them all why they were there.

I'm not jealous, she thought furiously. What is there to be jealous of? If Glenn Hunter wants to gaze adoringly at Jeannie and if she wants to flirt unashamedly, what's it to me?

'Hospital?' Jeannie said distractedly, reluctantly dragging her eyes away from Glenn. 'Oh, yes. He's fine. You won't believe this, but — ' She broke off grinning at them. 'Look, why don't you come inside. I'll make some coffee.'

She linked her arm through Glenn's and led the way into the house. Darcie, followed behind, said, 'I'll just wash my hands.'

In the bathroom, she closed the door and leaned against it, trying hard not to listen to Jeannie and Glenn's laughter. Why on earth had she said that she couldn't stand him when nothing could be further from the truth? Why not just deny there was anything between them? She scrubbed her hands and returned to the kitchen to find Jeannie and Glenn sitting at the huge, plank table.

'White, one sugar,' Jeannie said. 'Is that right?'

'Yes, thank you.' Darcie sat down and stared into her cup.

'Are you all right, Darcie?' Jeannie asked, concerned.

'Fine. About your dad . . . '

'Oh, yes, I was just telling Glenn.'

They exchanged looks and laughed. Darcie felt excluded, pushed out.

'Dad's fine. He called me yesterday to say he'd had a win with his premium bonds! One of the big prizes. Well, you know my dad. He thought he'd celebrate, so out came the rhubarb wine, and you know how potent that stuff is, at least, the way Dad makes it.'

Glenn was chuckling softly, shaking his head. Darcie felt the beginnings of a smile tug at the corners of her mouth. George Cooper's rhubarb wine was legendary in Horrington. One glass made you merry, two made you daft and any more than three rendered you unconscious! Or so the legend had it. She herself had never actually met anyone who risked more than two.

'He was drunk, Darcie! The daft old fella was drunk! Out cold on the kitchen floor. Mrs Burbridge called round for her eggs and milk and saw him sprawled out, so she called the police and an ambulance. Apparently . . . ' She broke off and wiped her eyes. 'Apparently, he started to come round in the ambulance and by the time they reached the hospital, he was in full voice and singing, 'I'm in the money!' at top blast.'

Swamped with relief, Darcie laughed. After the day she'd had, it was good to hear something funny.

'I'm sorry you two got called out. It was poor old Mrs Burbridge panicking. She assumed Dad had been out cold for days! Anyway, they're keeping him in to sleep it off. I've got to pick him up tomorrow.'

'Tomorrow?' Darcie said, surprised they were keeping him in so long.

'Mmm, they want to run some tests while they've got him,' Jeannie said, almost carelessly.

'Well, I don't know about you, but I'm famished,' Glenn said, having drained his cup. 'Would you ladies like to join me for lunch at The Plough?'

'Yummy!' Jeannie giggled, jumping to her feet. 'Show me the way! I'm starving.'

'Darcie?'

'I don't think so,' she said softly, feeling like a stick in the mud. 'I've left Philip on his own all morning. I should be getting back. He'll probably have to get back to college this afternoon.'

'Philip?' Jeannie cried. 'Oh, and who is Philip?' She nudged Glenn in the ribs and raised her eyebrows. 'Do I get a whiff of romance in the air?'

'He's a student!' Darcie protested.

'A student? Oh, Darcie, you are a dark horse.'

'But there's nothing . . . ' It was no use arguing. Jeannie just wasn't listening.

'Won't you be persuaded?' Glenn put his hand on her shoulder. 'You must be hungry, too. You've been working hard. I take back all I said about you being exhausted, by the way. You've proved the opposite today.'

She was tempted, but there was so much to be done. And she still had to break the news about Bernie to Philip. She shook her head.

'OK, I'll drop you off at your place on the way. If you're sure?'

She nodded, wishing he'd tried harder to persuade her.

★　★　★

Sitting in the back of the Land-Rover, Darcie felt almost as if she'd ceased to exist as Jeannie chattered non stop to Glenn. She and Jeannie had been friends since school. Jeannie was a bridesmaid at the wedding that never took place, and it was Jeannie who had mopped up Darcie's tears when it became clear that David wasn't going to turn up.

When the Land-Rover pulled up outside the sanctuary, she was torn between disappointment and relief.

'Sure you're all right?' Glenn asked as he helped her out of the vehicle. Was that real concern in his eyes, or was he just in a hurry to get rid of her so he could spend some time on his own with Jeannie? What do I care either way, she thought grimly.

'I'm fine!' she replied coolly. Glancing at the house, she saw Philip. He'd heard the car pull up and was waiting for her. 'Thanks, Glenn.'

She turned and hurried across the gravel, putting as much distance between herself and Glenn as possible. Philip looked at her, a mixture of hope and desperation in his eyes.

'I'm sorry, Philip,' she said, as gently

as she could. Reaching out, she put her hand on his arm. 'Bernie died under the anaesthetic.'

'Oh, Darcie!'

He fell against her and she found herself holding him in her arms. Poor lad. He'd been so fond of Bernie, they all had.

'It's all right, Philip,' she murmured soothingly, cradling his head against her shoulder. 'It was the best thing, really. You wouldn't have wanted him to go on suffering . . . '

She heard the door of the Land-Rover slam shut and the engine roar before Glenn drove off, spinning a shower of gravel in his wake.

Obviously he was in a desperate hurry to get away with Jeannie, she thought grimly. And who could blame him? Jeannie was a lovely, lively girl.

★ ★ ★

Darcie was exercising some of the dogs on the piece of land beside the sanctuary, deep in thought as she watched them race around happily.

'I should watch yourself, Miss Westbrook,' a horribly familiar voice said from behind. 'Very soon, you'll be a trespasser on this land and believe me, I'll have no compunction about seeing you prosecuted!'

Darcie turned around slowly, carefully composing her features into a look of controlled hostility.

'You have to buy the land first, Mr Harvey.'

'You obviously haven't heard the news,' he went on smugly. 'I've got my outline planning permission! Within a year, there'll be a whole new estate standing right where we are now, Miss Westbrook. If I don't get it, mark my words, some other builder will.'

She drew herself up, raised her chin and replied, 'Over my dead body.'

'Very courageous of you, Miss Westbrook.' He chuckled. 'But admit you're beaten. You haven't a hope of raising the money you'll need. I can afford to pay over the odds. The very fact that the land comes with planning permission has increased its value considerably.'

'Get lost!' she snapped and made to walk away, but his hand shot out and gripped her arm.

'I'd advise you to take your hand off me, Mr Harvey,' she said icily.

At last, Gifford Harvey dropped his hand, but his viperish smile was still there, still sickeningly smug. It had been a dreadful day so far, and this was all she needed to top it off.

Where are you when I really need you, Glenn Hunter, she wondered. Off with gorgeous Jeannie, enjoying lunch in The Plough no doubt!

No use tearing yourself apart wondering what he's getting up to, she decided. You've managed quite well without help so far.

'Admit it, Miss Westbrook. You know when you're beaten. You must have the best part of a quarter-acre there and I'm willing to pay a fair price for it.

What do you say?'

'Beaten?' Darcie said with a forced smile. 'I haven't even started to fight you yet, Mr Harvey!'

And with that, she turned on her heel and hurried off to round up the dogs.

Darcie was dozing in the chair in her living room when the telephone woke her.

'Hello,' she murmured sleepily and felt a little thrill race down her spine when she heard Glenn's voice.

'Is something wrong?'

'No, I just need to talk to you,' he said. 'I'm sorry to bother you so late . . .'

'What is it?' She tried to stifle a yawn and failed and heard him chuckle on the other end of the line.

'You're tired. It can wait until tomorrow. Will you have lunch with me? I'll pick you up at one. I can do my round when we get back.'

She was about to turn him down, but just as when she'd asked him to breakfast, her mouth charged ahead of her mind and she heard herself say, 'I'll be ready.'

'Tomorrow, then,' he said and hung up.

'Tomorrow,' she repeated and realised that she was smiling.

6

'You look lovely,' Philip remarked when Darcie appeared wearing a deep-blue, wool dress. She'd agonised for ages over what to wear, not wanting to appear too formal, yet loath to appear as if she hadn't bothered.

'You don't think it's too dressy for the Plough?'

'Not at all,' he said. 'You look great, honestly. I hope that Glenn Hunter knows how lucky he is.'

'It's not like that,' Darcie protested, but a sudden rush of heat colouring her cheeks belied the statement.

'Of course it isn't, Darcie,' Philip replied straightfaced.

She turned away and checked her reflection in the window. Should she have bothered putting her hair up? She'd left a few tendrils free to soften the look.

Then there was the make up. She didn't normally bother with much, but she'd taken ages over it today. She'd even used some of the perfume she saved for only the most special occasions.

'You reckon I'll do then?' she said.

Philip stared at her for a moment. 'You're daft, you are,' he said at last. 'Just because one guy was too stupid to know when he was on to a good thing, you think for some reason you're not worthy. Have confidence. Hold your head up, like yourself — '

'Is that him?' Darcie's heart went wild as she hurried to look out of the window. It wasn't his Land-Rover, but it was certainly Glenn climbing out of the silver Mercedes.

'Wow!' Philip whispered. 'Look at that car! I bet it goes like a bomb.'

But Darcie was looking at Glenn. He looked gorgeous, his long, lean legs encased in well-fitting, black trousers. The shirt he wore looked like black silk and a cream tie perfectly matched his tailored jacket.

'He looks like a gangster.' Philip laughed. 'Maybe you're not going to the Plough after all. Maybe you're going to rob a bank.'

Suddenly, Darcie was terrified that she didn't look good enough. The crisis of confidence came too late.

'I'll go and change,' she began, but there was no time, as the door was opening and Glenn was striding in.

His eyes took in every inch of her for several long seconds, his approval obvious, more so when he breathed, 'You look beautiful, Darcie.'

'Thank you,' she replied demurely, amazed that her voice could sound so normal when such turmoil was breaking loose inside her.

'Shall we go?' He held open the door and she walked through.

He closed the door, then hurried ahead to open the car passenger door for her. She nestled down in the soft, comfortable seat and closed her eyes.

'Is this your car?' she asked as he got in beside her.

'Of course,' he replied with a soft, throaty chuckle. 'What did you think?'

'I — I didn't know you had another.'

'You didn't think I'd take you out for lunch in the Land-Rover did you?'

He eased the car into gear and they slid soundlessly out of the drive and on to the road. Seconds later, they were passing the Plough.

'You've gone past the Plough,' she said.

'Yes,' he answered with a lop-sided grin. 'I know.'

'But — '

'Relax, Darcie. I'm not kidnapping you.'

He leaned forward and slid a tape into the player. At once, loud rock music began to blare out.

'Whoops!' he said sheepishly, ejecting the cassette with a jab of his finger. 'Wrong one!'

'I've nothing against rock,' she said as he slipped another tape in.

'I'm more in the mood for soul,' he said as Lionel Ritchie's warm voice filled the car.

Darcie turned her attention from the road and on to Glenn as he drove along. There was nothing she didn't like about him, from his dark, floppy hair to his wide, square jaw.

The lashes surrounding his blue eyes, were so dark that they appeared to have a line drawn around the base. His skin was smooth until you reached the jaw, then it was shadowed with stubble.

And she loved the way his wide mouth curved up at the corners, as if he was always ready to laugh. Although there were his brows, at odds with his mouth. Such dark, broody-looking things.

He turned to glance at her, making her jump.

'Penny for them?'

'Oh, I was just — just wondering where we're going. We seem to be heading out of town.'

'Hungry?' He laughed. 'Don't worry, we'll soon be there, Darcie, and you are in for a treat.'

She felt a tiny thrill as he turned the

car through the gates and on to a long, straight drive lined either side with golden and bronze leafed trees.

She'd heard that Horrington Hall had been converted into a country club housing one of the best and most famous restaurants for miles. Now she felt foolish for ever assuming that theirs would be a pub lunch!

Thank goodness I wore a dress, she thought as he pulled up outside the main entrance.

He hurried round to open the door for her and once she was out of the car, he took her hand, as if it were the most natural thing in the world, and led her up the steps.

'Good-afternoon, Mr Hunter.' A uniformed commissionaire opened the door for them and summoned the head waiter, who hurried across, his face wreathed in a welcoming smile.

'What I adore about this place, is it's old-world charm,' Glenn whispered in her ear. 'None of those ghastly revolving doors!'

'Your usual table by the window, sir.'

'Thank you, Michael,' Glenn said, taking over so that it was he and not the waiter who held Darcie's chair for her as she sank down on to a plush, red velvet seat.

'Like it?' he asked her, his eyes dancing as he sat down opposite.

'Like it, Glenn?' she repeated. 'I think it's lovely.'

She looked out of the window across the rolling countryside which even now, when autumn was coming to a close and winter was starting to bite, looked quite beautiful.

She wondered how Glenn could be so well known here when he'd only recently taken up his post in Horrington. Surely he hadn't become a regular patron here so soon.

'You'll find a wide selection of vegetarian meals on the menu,' he told her as the waiter handed them each a deep red folder.

Darcie opened hers and at once felt hunger pangs tear at her stomach. She hadn't had time for breakfast this morning and now she was ravenous.

She studied the menu for a few minutes until Glenn asked if she was ready to order, then he beckoned to the waiter who came over at once.

'Avocado and melon to start,' she said.

'Sir?'

He turned to Glenn.

'Deep fried mushrooms in chef's special creamy sauce,' he said. 'What about a main course, Darcie?'

'Ratatouille lasagne,' she said, her mouth watering already.

'I'll have the same, thank you, Michael,' Glenn said, closing the menu and handing it back. 'And a green salad, I think.'

'Do you normally eat vegetarian?' she asked.

'Occasionally,' he admitted. 'Lots of people do, without necessarily realising it. Quiche, pizza, risottos, they don't have to contain meat products.'

'Why today?'

'Darcie, sitting in your kitchen eating bacon you've cooked is one thing. I couldn't sit here with you now and tuck into a huge, juicy steak, knowing how you feel about it.'

'Some men think it's macho,' she remarked mischievously.

'Well, as you'll have gathered by now, I'm not some men, Darcie. I'm my own man and I do what's right, not what's expected of me. Anyway, let's change the subject and talk about you.'

'Me?'

'Tell me again about Eighty Acres and what your plans are for it.'

'You really wouldn't be interested.'

'Try me . . .'

* * *

The meal was delicious, but Darcie managed to find room afterwards for a generous slice of lemon cheesecake.

Every time Glenn laughed or spoke, it was like a soothing balm to her aching heart. Maybe, she thought with wild abandon, it's time to forget the past and admit to myself that David doesn't exist in every man.

'We'll have coffee in the lounge, Michael,' she heard Glenn's voice say and realised he was again holding her chair for her.

He led her through to a lounge overlooking the Italian garden and was settling her in a comfortable chair by the window, when a figure she recognised strode over.

'Glenn! I didn't expect to see you here today,' Lord Horrington boomed. 'And who is your lovely companion?'

'Darcie Westbrook,' Glenn said.

Darcie started to rise, but Lord Horrington motioned her to remain seated.

'The famous Miss Westbrook,' he said. 'I didn't recognise you for a moment. But, of course, we met at your fund-raising gala last summer.'

'That's right,' she said.

'Well, I won't intrude. I'll speak to you later, Glenn, regarding that matter we were discussing yesterday.'

'You've thought it over, Richard?'

'Suffice to say, I've decided in your favour. Do excuse me, Miss Westbrook, Glenn. It was delightful to meet you again.'

'First name terms with Lord Horrington,' Darcie exclaimed when he'd gone. 'You don't waste any time, do you, Glenn?'

He didn't answer, but sat regarding her with his deep blue eyes. She trembled inside. She wished he wouldn't look at her like that and yet — she didn't want him to stop either.

'We'll have to do this again,' he said.

'I'd like that,' she breathed. 'I've really enjoyed our lunch, Glenn.'

'Good.'

'Tell me about Lord Horrington,' she said. 'You obviously know him well. What made him turn this beautiful house into a country club?'

'Financial necessity is the short answer,' Glenn answered. 'The Horrington Corporation has its finger in several pies at the moment. It's quite a thriving business, covering everything from producing real fruit drinks to sport and leisure. And Fenn Farm, of course, remains the property of Lord Horrington.'

'You seem to know all about it,' she murmured.

'I'd rather know all about you,' he said, the gleam back in his eyes. 'Tell me all about Darcie Westbrook.'

'Nothing much to tell.' She smiled enigmatically.

'That's not what I've heard.'

She felt a prickle begin at the nape of her neck. Of course, it was too much to hope that Glenn hadn't been told of her very public humiliation.

'You've obviously heard that I was jilted,' she said coolly.

'It's an ugly word, Darcie. I could say the man was obviously a fool, but perhaps he wasn't. Better to find out before the wedding that you're about to make a mistake.'

'Could we talk about something

else?' she said bitterly.

'You should talk about it,' he urged. 'Don't keep it all bottled up inside. You've done nothing to be ashamed of.'

Stupid tears stabbed at her eyes. She hadn't cried over David in a long time, but having Glenn knowing all about what had happened somehow made everything that much more painful.

'I'm sorry,' he said gently. 'I didn't mean to upset you, Darcie.'

'You're forgiven,' she said with a small smile.

With a sudden sigh, he leaned forward.

'Time's getting on,' he said. 'I should be getting down to business.'

'Business?'

'My motive for taking you to lunch,' he explained, unaware that his words were like hammer blows to her heart. 'I have a proposition to put to you.'

Her mouth felt dry. She reached for the coffee pot and poured herself another cup, hardly able to stop her hands from shaking as she raised it to her lips.

A moment ago, he had raised the subject that had been the source of so much pain and hurt and now he wanted to talk business!

'What kind of proposition?' she asked when she was sure her voice wouldn't shake and let her down.

He was about to tell her when a waiter hurried over with an urgent message.

'Telephone, Mr Hunter.'

With a sigh of exasperation, Glenn apologised and hurried off, returning a few moments later.

'I'm so sorry, Darcie,' he said. 'I have to go. There's an emergency at one of the tenanted farms. Another horse has been attacked.'

Darcie gasped. She'd heard of such cruel and vicious attacks taking place all over the country. There had been one, the week before, which she had hoped was just a one off, but this new attack proved otherwise.

7

The following day, Darcie called at the vet's surgery to settle her account and was about to do so when Glenn appeared in reception.

'Darcie — over here,' he beckoned.

'What is it?'

'Ssh, just come with me. Quickly.'

Bemused, she followed him through the surgery area to Joe's living room. The mellow, golden, autumn sun gleamed through the windows, casting yellow light across the carpet where, right in the middle, lay Plato.

The kitten was on his back, rolling from one side to the other. He had a catnip mouse grasped between his front paws and was wildly kicking it with his back feet while Joe's cats looked on with disdain.

'He's grown!' Darcie whispered. 'He's almost doubled in size!'

'He's older than I first thought,' Glenn told her and as soon as the kitten heard his voice, he leaped to his feet, abandoning the catnip mouse and rushing on unsteady little legs towards them.

Glenn picked him up and rubbed noses with him, then the kitten scrambled to his shoulder and sat perched there like a furry parrot. Darcie reached up and tickled him and the loud purring became frantic and nasal.

'Great, isn't he?' Glenn said proudly. 'Although I don't think Joe's menagerie would agree. His collies take one look at Plato and vanish!'

'What about Thetis?'

'She's happy to stay at my house, lounging about in the conservatory all day! She seems afraid of the outside — and who can blame her after what she went through? She'll come out with me into the garden, but the minute I go inside, she rushes in after me.'

'It'll take time,' Darcie said. 'She just needs to build up her confidence.'

'I can wait,' he said, his eyes tender and Darcie had the awful, disquieting thought that he was talking about her and not the cat at all . . .

'Sergeant Greaves here,' came a familiar, slow voice when Darcie answered the telephone later that day. 'You'll know there have been some nasty attacks on horses locally and there's a call to set up a horsewatch scheme. I wondered if you'd be interested.'

'Certainly,' she said at once.

'Well, I've secured the use of the village hall tomorrow evening at seven. All welcome. I know it's short notice, but I'll be grateful if you could put the word round.'

'I'll do that, sergeant,' she said. 'Thank you for letting me know.'

'Well, we've got to do something about these attacks,' he went on. 'I've informed Mr Hunter — he said that he'd pick you up and give you a lift to the meeting.'

Darcie hung up the phone. Tomorrow was going to be a busy day, for in the morning it was the auction and she had to bid for Eighty Acres. And Glenn was coming to fetch her! Her heart gave a tiny flutter. Perhaps, she thought, perhaps he really did care . . .

The auction room was packed. Darcie had arrived early in order to secure a seat near the front, terrified that if she didn't, her bids might somehow go unnoticed. Most of the interest seemed to be in a small batch of repossessed houses and a barn complete with planning permission for a luxury conversion: At least, that's what Darcie hoped from the conversations she'd overheard.

Ten minutes before the auction was due to start, she felt a tap on her shoulder and turned to find herself looking right at Gifford Harvey. He was sucking on a fat cigar and wearing a rather shabby-looking sheepskin car coat.

'You might as well call it a day and go home now, Miss Westbrook,' he sneered. 'You're wasting your time here.'

'We'll see about that, Mr Harvey.'

Outwardly, she appeared very calm and collected, but inside she was a raging deluge of terror. Her stomach churned, the palms of her hands felt moist, but her mouth was dry and she longed for a drink.

She just hoped and prayed that when the moment came, her courage didn't fail her . . . What a ridiculous thought! She hadn't come this far to be let down by a foolish attack of nerves.

It was another hour before Eighty Acres came under the hammer.

The bidding was fast and furious and gradually, as the bids got higher, people dropped out until it was Darcie bidding against Gifford Harvey. She couldn't go much higher, but Gifford Harvey seemed quite at ease, as if he was willing to sit there all day until she gave up.

She kept on until she'd passed her limit and until commonsense told her she had to stop. She thought of that lovely piece of land crowded with more of Gifford Harvey's featureless little boxes. Where would she walk the dogs now? And what if the new residents complained and she was forced to close?

She was still fuming when she realised bidding was continuing. She turned, but in the crowd couldn't see who was bidding against Gifford Harvey. The man was looking distinctly uncomfortable now, not even sparing time for a triumphant glance in Darcie's direction.

At last, his face dark red, Gifford Harvey shook his head.

'Sold!' the auctioneer announced with a tap of his hammer. 'To the Horrington Corporation.'

★　★　★

Darcie waited, looking at her watch, looking out of the window, but there was no sign of Glenn.

'I'm going to have to go,' she told Annabel, a girl from the college who

115

had agreed to sanctuary-sit.

'He was most likely called out to an emergency,' Annabel remarked and Darcie wondered if she had really become so transparent.

'I doubt I'll find a parking space now and it's not far, so I'll walk. If Glenn Hunter turns up, tell him . . . '

Her voice trailed off and she shrugged. It was silly to feel so disappointed, so stood up!

Bright light spilled from the open doors of the village hall and several people gathered there. Darcie hurried over to join the others and turned just as Glenn Hunter drove up in his Land-Rover.

She felt pleased to see him until she saw who was sitting in the passenger seat. Jeannie!

Her face burned with humiliation. Not only had he stood her up, he'd then turned up with Jeannie. Quickly, before they could catch up with her, she dashed into the hall.

The hall was packed, all the seats

taken and several people stood along the back wall. On the rostrum, behind a long table, sat Sergeant Greaves and Mrs Carter. The whole horsewatch scheme was Mrs Carter's idea, one of her horses being the first victim. Glenn strolled in and took up the third chair on the rostrum beside Mrs Carter.

Mrs Carter spoke first, an impassioned speech which brought a heartfelt response from the audience.

Then it was Sergeant Greaves' turn to speak.

'I don't like the term vigilantes,' he began. 'If you're thinking of taking the law into your own hands, then I have to warn you straight away that you're going about things the wrong way. I'm all for the patrols that have been suggested, but I have to stress that if you see anything amiss, you must report it to the police. Apart from the fact that you could find yourselves in the wrong, these people — or person, whatever — are dangerous. I don't want any more casualties, equine — or human. Mr Hunter?'

Glenn stood and Darcie had to quell a shiver that ran the length of her spine. He spoke out confidently and clearly and had everyone listening with rapt attention, and no-one more than Darcie. She'd never expected to feel this way about a man again and now, looking back, wondered if she had ever really felt this deeply for David. It came as a shock to her to realise that all these years, what she had been nursing was injured pride rather than a broken heart.

But that couldn't be! She had loved David — hadn't she? Didn't her heart leap whenever he looked at her? Didn't her stomach turn over when he said her name? Didn't her knees turn to jelly at his touch?

The answer was no. She wasn't broken hearted, she was angry! Furious and outraged that David should have humiliated her in front of the whole village! It came to her in a blinding flash that her marriage to David would have been completely wrong. How lucky that David had realised in time. He'd tried to explain to her why he'd done what he did, but she'd been too hurt to listen.

And she'd gone on nursing that hurt ever since, confusing it with other emotions. David hadn't rejected her so much as the whole idea of marriage and commitment. He'd gone about it in the worst possible way, leaving it right up until the last moment, but if he hadn't . . .

Wasn't it possible that she could have found herself trapped in a loveless marriage? And what if she'd encountered Glenn Hunter under those circumstances?

The arguments were all academic, of course. Glenn wasn't interested. It was bright, vibrant Jeannie Cooper who had taken his eye.

'I've done a head count of those willing to participate in night patrols,' Glenn was saying. 'And if everyone is willing to give up one night's sleep

119

occasionally, we should have the area nicely covered. I suggest you sort yourselves into pairs, but make sure that at least one of you is capable of taking care of himself or herself,' he added, looking pointedly at a pair of young girls. 'I'll be patrolling with Miss Westbrook . . . '

Darcie felt as if she'd been thumped! Who on earth did he think he was, taking a decision like that? She hadn't agreed to patrol with him! How did he know she hadn't already decided to pair with someone? It seemed she hadn't got her message across yet that she was perfectly capable of taking care of herself.

As for dealing with the low-life that were attacking the horses, she was quite well equipped for that, having completed a self-defence course when she was eighteen.

'See Mrs Carter after the meeting and she'll organise the rota. If anyone can't make it, let her know and she'll assign someone else. And finally, remember what the sergeant said. These are dangerous, warped individuals. Don't take any unnecessary risks.' He smiled. 'Good luck.'

He came down from the rostrum and immediately sought Darcie out. She was fuming.

'How dare you?' she hissed. 'You sanctimonious . . .'

'I take it you don't want to patrol with me?' he said with a smile on his face that made her anger seem as silly as it was unwarranted.

'Of course I don't,' she cried. 'Why would I want to patrol with you of all people?'

'Why not?' he said, his tone still equable. 'I think we'd make a great team. Anyway, we're down on Barbara Carter's rota as a pair now, so unless you want to throw her schedule completely out of kilter — '

'You rat,' Darcie snarled.

'We've got a cracker of a night for our first patrol,' he went on. 'Guy Fawkes' night!'

'Well, since you have everything so

well arranged, I may as well go home. Good-night, Mr Hunter.'

She turned to go, but he grabbed her arm and swung her round to face him.

'Will you stop!' he said angrily, the thunder back in his eyes. 'What makes you so prickly? It's like trying to get acquainted with a porcupine! And what's all this about you going home? I'll take you.'

'I can walk, thank you.' She sniffed. 'I could use some fresh air.'

He dropped his hand from her arm. 'Now you're being plain stupid. I'll drive you home. Come on.'

It was dark and cold outside and everywhere was shrouded in an icy fog. Already regretting her hasty decision, Darcie pulled the collar of her jacket up and turned in the opposite direction to where Glenn's car was parked.

She heard his exasperated sigh, then, moments later, the roar of the engine as he started it up.

With a determined step, she started off up the hill. The fog was thick and soon her hair was plastered to her head and she just knew her cheeks would be black with mascara. Why did she bother? She should have known it was a mistake.

Walking along a narrow lane in the dark in thick fog was not the most intelligent thing to do, and she found herself wishing she'd done the sensible thing and accepted Glenn's offer of a lift.

Offer — it was more of an order and she didn't take orders from anyone! Least of all Glenn Hunter, she stormed silently. Just who did he think he was anyway? And what about Jeannie?

The Land-Rover slowed down beside her and Glenn leaned out.

'Will you stop acting the fool and get in,' he called over the noise of the engine. 'You're soaked through already and you're likely to be mown down in this thick fog.'

She ignored him and kept walking and the next time he pulled up in front of her.

'Get in!' he instructed.

'What about Jeannie?' she demanded. 'Won't she be waiting for a lift?'

He frowned, puzzled, then shook his head.

'She's not going home straight away. Look, is all this because I was late picking you up? I told Sergeant Greaves I'd bring you along, but how was I to know I'd get a panic stricken phone call from Jeannie?'

'I don't understand,' Darcie murmured, feeling rather foolish now.

'Well, if you'd listen occasionally instead of leaping to conclusions, you might know why I was delayed. One of the goats was having difficulties kidding and I went to lend a hand. I mentioned the meeting and Jeannie said she'd like to come along — just to get away from the farm, I think. She's sick to the back teeth with it, and with her father who won't do as he's been told and rest!'

'Oh,' Darcie mumbled, feeling stupid.

'Now will you stop being so damned stubborn and get in!'

The cold had finally reached her bones and, reluctantly, she complied.

He didn't speak at all on the journey home, but just as Darcie was getting out of the car, he said, 'Don't forget the fifth.'

He drove off, leaving her standing in the thick fog. He'd done it again! Tangled up all her emotions and left her to unravel the knots! And now she'd made things worse by having a stupid temper tantrum.

She wouldn't be surprised if he never wanted anything to do with her again!

8

'Hello,' Darcie said, with a welcoming smile. 'I wondered if I'd be seeing you here.'

She'd heard that the Strawson's cat had been put to sleep a couple of days before, and now here they were, the whole family.

Mr and Mrs Strawson entered the reception with their two children, a boy of about five and a girl a couple of years older.

Darcie could see at once that Mrs Strawson had been crying and knew that a couple of days wasn't a very long time to get over the loss of a beloved pet.

'Mr Nelson said you had some kittens,' Katie Strawson said.

'That's right,' Darcie beamed. 'Why don't you come down to the cattery.'

They seemed a little ill at ease, but

when she held out her hands to the children, they each clasped her hand and smiled up at her.

'I know you,' the little boy said. 'You helped me win a football at the gala.'

'So I did.' Darcie laughed. 'But don't tell anyone!'

'She was helping all the silly little kids,' the older sister said scathingly, rolling her eyes heavenwards. 'You couldn't have got the ball into the bucket on your own!'

'Could, too!'

'Before we go in,' Darcie said quickly, crouching down so she could look both children in the eyes, 'I must ask you to be very quiet. Some of the older cats in there are a little bit shy and nervous and big noises can alarm them.'

'We'll be quiet, Miss Westbrook,' the little girl said with an icy glare at her brother. 'Won't we, Matthew?'

'I'm always quiet,' he said angelically, then grinned a gappy grin that melted Darcie's heart. She ruffled his untidy, fair hair and opened the door.

As a precaution against escape, there was a double door system on the cattery and it took a while to get the five of them in.

Once inside, the children quickly found their feet and with a gentle reminder from their mother to be quiet, they peered in the pens. Darcie watched the family carefully. She wanted to be one hundred per cent sure that this was what they all wanted. It was no good the children wanting a kitten, if the parents were reluctant.

'We've got three litters at present,' she explained. 'These are just two weeks old, those over there are four weeks, but the ones in the end pen are coming up to eight weeks. There are adult cats, too, of course,' she added.

'Look at this one, Mummy!' the little boy called. 'Isn't he lovely?'

In the end pen, the older kittens had all come to the wire door to gaze curiously at the visitors. Darcie barely noticed the whispering of the doors as they opened and closed behind her.

'I'm not sure,' Mrs Strawson said, keeping her voice low. 'I'm just not sure. I'm so afraid — I love cats, well, all animals really. It's just it hurts so much when you lose them and we've lost two in the last few months.'

Mr Strawson was with the children, holding the younger one up so he could see properly into the pen. Darcie was impressed with their behaviour. A lot of children wouldn't have been so quiet and restrained.

'It's so hard to tell a child that their beloved pet had to die,' Mrs Strawson went on. 'We had a burial service in the garden. The children stroked Jet, said goodbye, then we put him in a box and buried him.'

Tears welled in her eyes and she let them spill. Darcie rested a comforting hand on her arm and drew her gently to one side. She knew exactly how she felt and knew that words didn't exist that would make everything right again. Only time would heal these particular wounds, time and patience and perhaps the love of another pet.

Darcie said gently, 'Children need to be able to grieve, too. It can be eased if they're allowed to see the body and say goodbye. Some people think that it's macabre, but it can be quite poignant and it helps them to understand that the pet has really died.'

Mrs Strawson blew her nose and smiled fondly at her husband and children.

'Look at them.' She sighed. 'I can hardly say no to them now, can I? Part of me wants to say, no more animals, it hurts too much when they die, and we've lost two in the past six months, but — '

'Mummy, can we have this one?' Matthew called. 'He's lovely. Please, Mummy. He's got beautiful blue eyes.'

'No, this one, Mummy,' Emily, the older of the two children protested. 'She's so pretty.'

Still Mrs Strawson hesitated. If Darcie doubted for one moment that the Strawsons would give a loving home to a pet, she wouldn't entertain them.

'Having a kitten to care for could ease some of the pain — for all of you,' Darcie said. 'You can't ever hope to replace the cats you've lost, but a new little individual with a personality and character all of his own could fill that awful, empty space in your heart.'

'I do miss having a cat around the house. You get used to them, don't you?' Mrs Strawson whispered.

'I don't think fear of being hurt by their death is a good enough reason not to have another pet,' Darcie said. 'They give so much back in return for regular meals and love. I think you should give it another chance, Mrs Strawson, really I do.'

'You're right, of course,' the woman replied. 'Just because we've been unlucky twice, doesn't mean there has to be a third time, whatever the old wives might say. And who knows, perhaps there's a way of breaking that old saying that bad things happen in threes!'

She was smiling brightly and hurried forward to join her husband and children at the pen.

'I'll open it so you can cuddle them,' Darcie said.

'That's the one I want!' Matthew cried as Darcie lifted out a black and white kitten with four white socks and a white tip to his tail. 'I'll call him Tip!'

'He's a she, Matthew,' Darcie said, crouching down and carefully passing the kitten to the little boy. 'Hold her like this . . . that's right. Good boy. She likes you . . . can you hear her purring?'

In her experience, kittens were expert at choosing exactly who they wanted to live with and there was no doubt that the little black and white kitten had chosen Matthew for her special person. The little girl was staring at the black kitten she'd picked out.

Darcie handed it to her. 'She's so cute,' Emily said, gently nuzzling the back of the kitten's head with her nose. 'Oh, please, Mummy, can't we have this one? I'd call her Inky.'

She was Darcie's particular favourite in this litter, a fuzzy, black ball with long grey hairs on her back legs.

'Perhaps Mummy would rather choose,' Darcie suggested.

'She looks just like Jet when we first got him,' Mrs Strawson choked. 'Exactly the same. It could be the same cat.'

She blinked back tears and looked at the other kittens in the pen. They'd lost interest in the visitors and had decided to pester their mother.

'But I like this one, Mummy!' Matthew protested, tears gathering in his eyes. 'Why do we always have to do what she wants?'

'Matthew, don't start that, or you might frighten the kittens. Remember, they're still only babies,' Mrs Strawson scolded.

'Sorry,' he whispered, kissing the top of the kitten's head. 'But I love her. I really, really love her. Please, Mummy . . . Oh, please can't we have this one?'

Darcie could feel her own heart

strings being tugged mercilessly, so only heaven knew how poor Katie Strawson must be feeling right now.

'I'm with Matthew on this one, love,' Mr Strawson said. 'We can't ever hope to replace Jet with a look-a-like and this little lady is rather sweet.'

Darcie could see the parents were being torn two ways. Gently she eased Mrs Strawson to one side and whispered, 'Why not take both?'

'Both?'

'You had two cats before, didn't you?'

'Well, yes, we did,' Mrs Strawson considered. 'We had two so they'd be company for each other. It simply hadn't occurred to me to get a pair again! Thank you, Miss Westbrook! You're brilliant.'

She turned around. The children were glaring at each other, each clutching the kitten they'd chosen.

'We'll have both,' Mrs Strawson announced.

'Both!' Mr Strawson cried, but he looked far from displeased. 'Your idea, Miss Westbrook?'

'It's the logical solution,' she said, laughing off her involvement. 'You'd probably have thought of it yourselves, given time.'

'Can we take them with us now?'

'I don't see why not. I usually wait until they're eight weeks old, but as they're only a few days off and these are exceptional circumstances . . . '

It was days like this that made everything worthwhile for Darcie. Seeing animals going to loving, responsible homes, knowing they'd receive as much love as they gave.

'I'll give you a starter pack with food, leaflets about vaccinations, worming and general care,' she said briskly as she closed the pen again. The mother cat looked unconcerned that two of her offspring were no longer with her. It would probably be a relief for her to be rid of them!

She turned to go to the large storage area at the end of the cattery where she kept the starter packs she'd mentioned and almost bumped into Glenn.

'What are you doing here?' she hissed. 'Why are you hiding and how did you get in?'

'Through the door, same as you,' he drawled. 'Well done, Darcie. Some satisfied customers there I think. And that was some handsome advice you were dishing out.'

'Handsome?'

'All that about giving love a second chance.'

'Love was never mentioned,' she muttered under her breath, and grabbed a box from the shelf, checking through its contents.

'I can let you borrow a pet carrier if you need one,' she said, turning back to the family who were now coming towards her.

'It's all right, Miss Westbrook, thank you all the same,' Mrs Strawson said. 'We haven't far to go. They can sit with the children in the back of the car.'

'What about payment?' Mr Strawson asked. 'We can't take all this without giving you something.'

'I usually ask for a donation,' Darcie said. 'Whatever you can afford.'

Mr Strawson reached into his pocket and took out his cheque book.

'Have you a pen, Miss Westbrook?'

'In the office,' she said smiling.

When they'd gone, she accompanied Glenn on his rounds and he was his usual cheerful self. It would be so easy to drop her defences, but dare she? She'd already been hurt once. Did she really want to risk it all over again? And there was Jeannie of course, who just seemed to have to crook her little finger to have him running . . .

When he'd finished, she went into the kitchen with her and sat down with a cup of coffee.

'Now we're on our own, I'd like to talk to you,' he said. 'Goodness knows, I've been trying to find the opportunity long enough.'

'What about?' Her heart was beating like a drum.

'It's about . . . ' he began and was cut short by his mobile phone. 'Blast!'

Once again, he was summoned away to an emergency, only this time before leaving, he dropped a kiss on her forehead and said, 'We will have to talk — one way or another!'

★　★　★

It was quiet in the sanctuary that afternoon, and Darcie was delighted when Betty came in with Mandy.

'Hello, dear! I just thought I'd pop in to see if there was any news of the kitten,' Betty said.

'You wouldn't recognise him, Betty,' Darcie told her cheerfully. 'He's a plump, active bundle of mischief!'

'I'm so glad.' Betty smiled. 'I've just been to see Glenn. He fixed up Mandy's leg a treat. She doesn't worry about it at all now.'

Darcie invited the old lady to sit down and have a cup of tea.

'Betty, are you managing at the cottage?'

'Well, I am and I'm not,' she said.

'Some days are good, others — not so good. I'll give it a bit longer, then I'll think about going into sheltered housing.'

'If it's Mandy that's worrying you, there are places that don't mind you keeping pets.'

'Really?' Betty perked up. 'Oh, if I could take Mandy, I'd be out of that draughty, old cottage like a shot.'

'I'm sure there are some empty units at Spring Meadows. Why don't you call in and see them? They're all very nice there.'

'You know, I might call in on my way home from here,' Betty said thoughtfully. 'Thank you, Darcie. Now, enough about me, what about you?'

'What about me?' Darcie laughed.

'You and that handsome, young vet of course!' Betty cackled.

'Oh, Betty,' Darcie shook her head slowly. 'I really don't know.'

'You enjoy yourself, my dear! He's a lovely, young man. You deserve some happiness.'

Joe Nelson appeared next day to make the round of the sanctuary.

'Nice and quiet this afternoon,' he remarked as he cleaned his hands after being round all the pens.

Darcie was disappointed that Glenn hadn't come, but pleased to see Joe none the less.

'So what's all this I hear about you and Glenn?' Joe asked with a twinkle in his eye.

'You've been talking to Betty, haven't you?'

'Since your wedding day fiasco, I've watched you withdraw further and further into yourself. Several young men have tried to break down those defences of yours and so far, none has succeeded.'

'Perhaps they don't try hard enough,' she teased.

'It's no laughing matter, Darcie,' he began, then broke off. His cheeks puffed out as he smiled. He'd always reminded Darcie of Father Christmas with his jolly smile and constantly laughing eyes. 'Is this advice coming a little too late?'

'Glenn and I are pairing off for the horsewatch thing, that's all.'

'And you're as pleased as punch to be going?'

'Mixed feelings,' she admitted. 'He seems decent . . . '

'Then he must have spoken to you about Eighty Acres?' Joe said.

'What about it?'

'That the Horrington Corporation has bought it and plan to open a riding centre for the disabled there. Didn't you know?'

'No,' she said softly. 'I didn't know. What else is intended for the land, Joe?'

A sudden, icy cold spear, penetrated the warm glow surrounding her heart.

'It's for Glenn to tell you,' he said. 'I thought he would have done by now.'

'Tell me what? Joe, what's going on? What does Glenn have to do with Eighty Acres?'

'He'll tell you that himself, my dear,

when he's ready.'

No matter how Darcie pressed, Joe refused to say any more than that. What could it be? What secrets did he have? Had she been premature in letting her defences drop?

Towards the end of Glenn's afternoon surgery, as things were beginning to calm down after the early rush and just as Glenn was about to see his last patient, the door was thrown open and Darcie rushed in cradling something in her arms.

'Glenn!' Darcie cried. 'It's Puss!'

'What happened?'

'There was a lorry reversing into the drive — Puss didn't move out of the way fast enough.'

Glenn's mind was whirling. He looked at the pathetic, limp, black bundle lying in Darcie's arms. He was barely conscious. He'd a soft spot for the cat himself and he knew how much Puss meant to Darcie.

'Bring him through to the treatment room,' he said quickly, not even attempting to lift him from Darcie's arms.

If anything happened to Puss . . .

He was a once in a lifetime cat. There was a special bond between Darcie and Puss that went far beyond a normal pet/owner relationship. Glenn knew it and knew he had to save the cat at all costs.

'Glenn . . . ' she said, her eyes pleading as she entered the surgery.

'Ruth can assist me if you . . . '

'No,' she said firmly. 'I want to stay with him.'

'Gently does it,' Glenn murmured as Darcie lowered Puss on to the table.

'It all happened so quickly,' she said. 'There was nothing the driver could do. He won't die, will he, Glenn?'

'He won't die, Darcie,' Glenn said gently. 'Not if I can help it.'

Heart thumping, Darcie stood beside Glenn as he examined Puss. Tears kept filling her eyes as she stroked the soft head and whispered words of comfort, but she blinked them back. There would be time for tears later, when the job was done, but right now, Puss needed her and she couldn't let him down.

'Sure you're all right for this?'

Glenn glanced up at her and again she saw the tenderness in his eyes. Her heart turned over. He really cared about what happened to her, about her feelings. She couldn't speak, only nod.

The tail hung limp and lifeless and there was no response, not even a flicker, when Glenn nipped it and Darcie's heart sank. He did the same to both hind legs, nipping the web of skin between the toes.

'Broken spine?' she whispered fearfully.

'I don't think so.' Gently he ran his fingers along the length of the spine. 'I certainly can't feel any damage. I suspect he's broken his pelvis. We'll get him X-rayed. I'm pretty sure there's a break in his right foreleg as well.'

Darcie let out her breath in a long sigh. Then were was hope! Puss looked up at her, his green eyes filled with trust. The look nearly broke her heart. Glenn's voice, brusque and coolly professional, broke into her thoughts.

'Darcie, you can assist with the X-ray. I'm going to knock him out and set that leg.'

She turned herself to automatic pilot and got everything ready for Glenn to operate.

Afterwards, she couldn't remember a thing she'd done, for she had trusted herself wholly to instinct and memory. Her mind was totally on Puss. He'd been her constant companion from the time he'd been given to her as a weak, three-week-old, orphaned kitten, the only survivor of a half-wild litter. He'd had that same look about him as Plato, the look that said he wanted to live.

He couldn't be in better care, she knew that. If there was the slightest chance Puss would survive all this, then it was in Glenn's capable hands.

The X-ray confirmed Glenn's diagnosis.

'I'll operate straight away,' Glenn said briskly.

Darcie watched as Glenn clipped the fur on the cat's foreleg and inserted a needle into the vein, steadily injecting the anaesthetic.

'Get him connected up to the gas machine, Darcie. I'm just going to set that leg.'

'What about the pelvic fracture?'

'Just a crack, Darcie. It'll heal better on it's own with plenty of cage rest.' His brief smile was both encouraging and reassuring. 'Try not to worry, love. He'll pull through.'

She watched him work, his long, deft fingers so gentle, yet so strong. He was so different from David. David was a businessman, first and foremost. He dealt in money, property, anything likely to make him a tidy profit. Perhaps, in the end, he feared Darcie wouldn't be a viable proposition. Perhaps he thought he'd do better married to the daughter of some wealthy property magnate!

Vets were different, more interested in their work than making money — at least, vets like Joe Nelson and Glenn Hunter were.

'Penny for them, Darcie?' Glenn asked out of the blue. 'You were miles away, love.'

'Oh, I was just thinking how good you are at your job,' she answered truthfully. 'Did you always want to be a vet?'

'Always,' he said. 'Ever since I was a little boy. I wasn't allowed pets at home, so I used to look after the class pets at school! My father thought I was crazy!'

'What does he think of you now?'

'My father's dead,' he replied shortly, the sudden ice in his tone stinging Darcie. 'Right, that's him done. I'll keep him sedated for a while, give that pelvis a chance to start healing. You're going to have to keep him caged for a while, Darcie.'

'I know,' she said ruefully. 'He's not going to like that.'

'We'll keep him warm. I'll put in a

drip and we'll do half-hourly observations for two hours, then hourly after that.'

They got Puss settled, then Glenn turned to look at Darcie. 'I'm sorry about earlier,' he said, flicking his hair back from his eyes. 'Snapping at you about my father. You weren't to know.'

She shrugged and walked back towards him. 'What is there to know?'

'There was no love lost between us. We weren't even speaking when he died. Or rather, he wasn't speaking to me. He could never accept that I wanted to live my life my way and not his. My mother died when I was small and there was just me and Dad all those years — '

He broke off and Darcie could see the pain in his eyes. She had never even considered that behind his cheerful smile, he could be nursing such hurt. Perhaps that explained his quick temper and his knotty eyebrows!

'You'd have thought it would have

made us close, but it didn't. We were always at loggerheads. I tried to make it up with him, but the last time I saw him, he said he never wanted to see me again. As far as he was concerned, his only son died along with his wife.'

'That's terrible,' Darcie cried. 'What an awful thing to say.'

'He was a proud man, Darcie. I found out after he'd died that he wanted to make his peace with me, but just didn't know how. Still, you can't change the past, can you?'

He was looking at her questioningly and she felt the colour flood into her face.

'You mean David,' she whispered.

'You'll never change what happened, love, but you can learn to accept it and perhaps, one day, to see it was for the best.'

He was right of course. She grabbed her bag, said goodbye and hurried out to her car. But instead of going straight home, she made a detour and stopped outside the Norman church in which she and David should have been married.

It all seemed so long ago now, so far away. Looking back, it was almost as if it had happened to someone else. Her grandmother's house, packed to the rafters with wedding gifts and wall-to-wall relations! Her parents and sister, Gabby, flying in from Australia for the occasion. The ivory, pure-silk wedding dress made specially for her . . .

She remembered her father, sitting beside her in the carriage, his back as straight as a board as they trotted through the village. It had been like a royal occasion with people lining the streets, waving, cheering her on her way.

In that awful moment, when it became clear that David had no intention of turning up, she'd been overwhelmed with anger, so consuming, it had completely taken over her life.

And as the days and weeks passed, instead of easing, the anger intensified.

She gazed out of the window at the ancient bricks, mellowed by the dying sun, and knew it was over.

The anger, the pain . . . gone. David didn't matter any more. He was in the past, over with and finished. She had a new life to look forward to and wouldn't waste another moment on regret.

With a smile on her face, she started the car and headed home.

9

'Dad's resting,' Jeannie said as she polished the white kitchen tiles. 'I'm determined to have this place as neat as a pin for him! He's in a right old mood having to be resting in bed, but I kept telling him, it was his own fault. Anyway, all the tests they did didn't show up anything worrying.'

Darcie had finally given in to Jeannie's demands to come for a visit, demands which had become more frantic since her father's discharge from hospital. He wasn't, Darcie gathered, the most compliant of patients!

'This place is driving me up the wall,' Jeannie complained. 'I never liked living here when I was a kid — I like it even less now! Did I hear a car?'

Darcie looked out of the window and saw Glenn's Land-Rover coming down the drive and her heart began to pound.

'What's Glenn doing here?'

'Oh, it's him, good. Yes, I want him to have a look at one of the goats.'

Darcie went outside with Jeannie and wondered if the pleased look on Glenn's face was for her or for her friend.

'You look pretty, Darcie,' he remarked with a smile. 'Very pretty.'

Darcie flushed and turned away in case Jeannie saw. To Jeannie he said, 'Now, where's this goat?'

'Em — over here — in the shed,' Jeannie said, casting puzzled glances at Darcie. 'I haven't dared tell my dad she's so sick. He blames me for everything that goes wrong around here anyway!'

Glenn's jaw tightened as he examined the sick goat.

'What on earth have you been feeding her on, Jeannie?'

'The usual,' she replied with a shrug. 'But that one got into Dad's compost heap and ate her way through a load of mouldy greens. I thought she'd just have a bit of belly ache, but then this happened.'

'Thank goodness she's not one of the pregnant ones. How long has she been down?'

'She was still on her feet when I called you, but she was having trouble breathing. Is it serious, Glenn?'

He ignored her question and turned to look at Darcie. 'My bag, Darcie!'

She opened his bag and, turning, Glenn rummaged through and brought out a long, sharp knife.

'What are you going to do?' Jeannie cried.

'Hopefully save her life,' Glenn grated furiously. 'See if you can comfort her, Darcie — '

'I'll be all right,' Jeannie whispered shakily.

'Not you — the goat!' he barked.

Darcie hunkered down on the hay beside the goat and stroked her head.

'She's barely breathing, Glenn. The pressure inside must be intense.'

'Here goes then,' he replied shortly

and measuring the correct distance with his fingers, plunged the knife into the goat's left side, releasing the putrid contents of the stomach and the agonising pressure at the same time.

Almost immediately, the goat's breathing became easier and the animal's relief was obvious.

'Glenn,' Darcie whispered urgently. 'It's Jeannie — I think she's going to faint!'

'Better look after her,' he said briskly. 'I'll finish off in here.'

He broke off and looked regretfully at Darcie's dress as she hurried to her feet and over to her friend. She'd looked so pretty when he arrived — like a girl for once! And now she was all messy.

'Come along,' Darcie said tersely. 'I'll get cleaned up, then I'll make us all a cup of tea.'

'She will be all right, won't she?' Jeannie whispered, leaning heavily on Darcie as they walked back towards the house. 'Dad'll kill me if he finds out what a mess I've made of things. I'm just not cut out for this. I'll be glad when Lee gets here . . . '

'Your brother? He's coming home?'

'Bringing his wife and their children,' she said. 'They're going to move in with Dad and Lee's going to help run the place. He lost his job some time ago and he can't find another. It seemed the logical solution as he's always been more at home with this sort of thing than me.'

Darcie was relieved, if only for the sake of the animals.

'What about Glenn?' she had to ask. 'What does he think about you leaving?'

Jeannie shrugged. 'He probably thinks it's just as well given my track record. I don't think I've made a very good impression there, Darcie, not like you!'

There was a mischievous twinkle in Jeannie's eye when she said that.

They entered the warm kitchen and found George waiting for them in his dressing-gown.

'What's going on?' he demanded.

'Why have you called the vet out again, Jeannie?'

He looked at Darcie's dress and immediately knew what had happened.

'Bloat!' he said. 'How could you let it happen, Jeannie?'

'It wasn't Jeannie's fault,' Darcie put in quickly. 'The goat managed to get into your compost heap.'

'She's all right now?' he asked. 'Oh, never mind, I'll see for myself.'

He grabbed his coat from the back of the kitchen door and went out, grumbling all the way.

'You'd better come upstairs,' Jeannie said. 'I'll see if I can find you some clean clothes to wear.'

Darcie, freshly washed, slipped into the shirt and jeans Jeannie had loaned her. The dress had been a mistake, but she'd just wanted to dress herself up for a change, to be feminine and . . .

'It's ruined,' Jeannie said, holding Darcie's stinking dress at arm's length. 'I shouldn't think any self-respecting dry cleaner will touch it smelling like that! How did you ever stand working for a vet?'

Jeannie pushed Darcie's dress into a plastic carrier bag.

'I thought you said you couldn't stand Glenn Hunter, Darcie? I saw the way you looked at him out there in the goat shed! And the way he looked at you. There is something going on between you two, isn't there?'

'We get on all right,' Darcie said non-commitally. 'He's all right.'

Jeannie sat down on the bed behind Darcie and looked at their reflections in the mirror. 'I never thought you'd want to speak to him again after what happened.'

'What was that?' Darcie frowned. She had no idea what Jeannie was talking about, but a strange chill had started deep inside. She remembered what Joe had said about Eighty Acres and how she had pushed it to the back of her mind.

'Well, he bought Eighty Acres, didn't he?'

'No.' Darcie laughed. 'Lord Horrington bought it.'

'No, Darcie, the Horrington Corporation bought it,' Jeannie corrected her. 'That's Lord Horrington and Glenn Hunter. Surely you knew? It was Glenn who saved Horrington Hall.'

'No,' Darcie whispered. Surely this couldn't be so. How could Glenn buy the land and not tell her? And what did he want it for?

'He's a whizz at making money — takes after his father for that, I believe,' Jeannie went on. 'He was a big property developer and when he died, he left Glenn a small fortune . . . '

Darcie spun round so she could face Jeannie. Her heart was thundering so fast, so hard, she felt sure it could be heard.

'You must have known,' Jeannie said weakly. 'Surely he told you?'

Darcie's silence was all the answer Jeannie needed.

'Me and my big mouth,' she groaned. 'Why did he buy the land, Jeannie?'

Darcie asked urgently. 'You seem to know all about it.'

'They're going to use a few acres to set up a riding centre for the disabled. As to the rest — ' She broke off and bit her lip. 'When I asked, he said he had plans for it. His father was a property developer, Darcie. He's got connections in the building world so perhaps . . . '

The last of Darcie's hopes came crashing around her. Glenn had deceived her. All the time he'd wanted Eighty Acres for himself and all his sweet talk . . . Wasn't it obvious? He was after her property as well! How could she let herself be used like that? How could she fall into that same tender trap all over again?

At least this time, she hadn't quite made it to the altar! She got to her feet, turned and stormed downstairs where Glenn was sitting in the kitchen chatting to George. He looked up as she entered and grinned his heart-stopping grin. But Darcie's heart was as cold as ice and nothing could melt it.

'I'm going home!' she snapped.

'I'm sorry about the dress, Darcie,' Glenn began, assuming that was the reason for her anger.

'How dare you lie to me?' she cried. 'Why didn't you tell me you owned the Horrington Corporation?'

'Fifty-one per cent actually,' he drawled. 'What of it? Is that what this is about?'

How could he be so calm, so matter of fact when he was solely responsible for breaking her so recently mended heart?

'You lied to me!'

'No, I didn't. I never lied to you,' he rejoined. 'I've been waiting for the right moment to tell you . . . '

'Well, you're not having my house or my land!' she cried. 'Over my dead body, Glenn Hunter! You'll never get your hands on it while I live and breathe . . . '

'I don't want your land, Darcie.' A note of exasperation had crept into his voice now. He didn't sound nearly so sure of himself. 'You've got it all wrong.'

'No, you've got it wrong. You've got me wrong! You're just another Gifford Harvey. A sheep in wolf's clothing!'

'Don't you mean a wolf in sheep's clothing?' He laughed softly, his laughter fanning the flames of her anger. 'Darcie, if you'll just let me explain, I — '

She flung the door open and stormed out of the house and over to her little car. He ran behind her, grabbed her, swung her round to face him.

'Don't touch me!' she wrenched her arm away.

'Listen to me!'

'No, I won't listen to you. I never want to see you again, not ever!'

His face was dark with anger, his eyebrows almost meeting across the top of his nose.

'Do you always have to be so damned hostile?' he said, his voice low, but charged with anger. 'Aren't you prepared to give me a fair hearing?'

162

'You lied to me.' She repeated her earlier accusation.

'I never lied to you! Not once. Every time I've been about to tell you my plans for Eighty Acres, something's happened — '

'Oh, how very convenient for you.'

She swung round on her heel and this time, as she headed for the car, he didn't follow. As she plunged her key into the lock and twisted it, she heard the Mercedes engine being gunned. They sped off at the same time, but in different directions.

Back home she ran a deep bath determined to soak all her troubles away.

It wasn't until she was soaking in the foam, the warm, soft water caressing her body, that she allowed herself a single thought about Glenn Hunter. Not the man who had lied to her and deceived her, but the man she had fallen in love with. The man she still loved and would probably go on loving until the end of time.

'It ends here,' she whispered and the tears she'd been holding back since the moment Jeannie told her the truth began to stream down her face until mascara ran into her eyes, blinding her and her throat felt hard and dry.

She allowed herself this release, as if her tears could wash Glenn Hunter out of her system and drive him away from her mind for ever. She cried until she could cry no more, then she climbed out of the water and dried herself on a warm towel. There was a spiritless and ice-cold hand clutching her heart in its frigid grip.

She would never cry for Glenn Hunter again because she would never feel for him again — for anyone. She had been a fool ever to allow herself the comfort of doing so, for the brief joy it had brought to her soul was not worth the grief she now felt.

Over the next few days, Darcie managed quite adeptly to avoid any contact with Glenn Hunter.

Puss was home, confined still to a

cage and not at all happy about it, but Darcie could see him growing stronger every day and knew his imprisonment wouldn't last very much longer. Unlike her own self-imposed imprisonment which would last for the rest of her life.

Glenn, wisely, seemed to be keeping out of her way, his visits to the sanctuary usually taking place when she was busy. Their brief exchanges were always to the point and achingly polite. Occasionally, she'd catch him watching her and, at times, it was nearly enough to dissolve her steely resolve, but she always caught herself in time, before she surrendered to those tender, blue eyes that disguised a heart of iron.

The man was a puzzle. Why did someone with so much money, and such an obvious talent for making more of it, waste his time being a vet? She couldn't make him out, and every time she tried to fathom it, she'd catch herself and turn her mind to other matters. She didn't want to figure him out. He was a closed book. She'd read the last page and there was no point opening it again.

★ ★ ★

On the night of November fifth, Darcie and Philip checked that all the animals were secure. There shouldn't be any fireworks near the sanctuary, but one never knew and Darcie always took adequate precautions. Everything done, they stood outside in the clear, frosty night and looked up at the stars twinkling in the sky overhead.

'It's a great night for fireworks,' Darcie commented. 'When we were young, it always seemed to be either raining or blowing a gale on Guy Fawkes' Night.'

'Who's that?' Philip said as they heard a car crunching over the gravel at the front of the house. 'At this time of night.'

'Probably someone bringing an animal in,' Darcie said. 'I'll see to it.'

She got to the front door before the

bell rang and opened it to find herself face to face with Glenn Hunter.

'What do you want?' she breathed.

'It's November fifth,' he said lazily.

'What about it?' Darcie said coldly.

'Our night to patrol. Horsewatch — remember? Or are you going to let me down on that, too?'

'Me — let you down?' she cried. 'You've got a nerve!'

His face broke into a smile. 'Does that mean you're coming along?'

'Of course,' she said. 'I'll just get my gloves and tell Philip. When do you think we'll be finished?'

'Dawn.'

'Dawn,' she repeated, swallowing hard. She wasn't worried about spending a whole night patrolling, but she was terrified at the thought of spending all those hours with Glenn.

When she'd fetched her gloves, she returned to find him waiting in his Land-Rover. She climbed in beside him and he immediately shone a powerful torch on a map he had propped against the steering-wheel.

'We'll park here, here, here and here,' he said, tapping the map with his finger. 'Have you got decent walking shoes on?'

'Of course.'

Being this close to him was assassinating her resolve. She couldn't stand it, not for an entire night! She'd be a nervous wreck by the end of it.

'Good, well we'll walk out these areas, then return to the car and drive on to the next.'

He folded the map and handed it and the torch to Darcie.

'How's Puss?' he asked.

'Recovering,' she replied. 'Plato and Thetis?'

'Thriving,' he answered.

He started the Land-Rover and drove to their first stopping point. Glenn planned to walk the footpaths that wound through the fields where several horses were kept. Several of the animals had retired into their shelters for the night, but a few remained, their silhouettes clearly visible in the brilliant moonlight. Like sitting ducks, Darcie thought grimly.

She spoke without thinking, her voice almost friendly. 'Have the other patrols had any luck?'

'Yes. So far they've managed to prevent two attacks, disturbing them just as they were about to get into the fields. There are two of them and they can run pretty fast!'

'What makes them do something like that?' Darcie said.

It had always been beyond her understanding how anyone could hurt an animal. There was no reason as far as she could see, for inflicting harm or pain on another living creature.

'Twisted, warped minds?' Glenn shrugged. 'I don't know. Presumably they get some kind of sick kick out of it, although Sergeant Greaves has a theory and I must say, it holds water.'

'Go on,' she said, her interest kindled.

'Every time there's one of these

attacks, a robbery takes place soon after. The sergeant thinks they deliberately tie his time up, so they can get on with their real business without worrying too much about him turning up.'

'Is that possible?'

'Anything's possible. It would be nice to think they at least had some kind of motive and weren't just doing it for kicks.'

'It doesn't make any difference why they're doing it,' Darcie said vehemently. 'They're evil.'

'I agree. That's why we're going to catch them!'

'Us?'

'Perhaps not us, but one of the patrols. Eventually they're bound to come across someone who can run as fast as them!'

They completed the circuit of the field and returned to the Land-Rover.

Darcie's heart hadn't done a single normal beat since the moment she'd opened her door to find Glenn standing there. And now she was sitting beside

170

him again, breathing in the familiar smell of his cologne, watching his big, capable hands on the wheel as he drove through the lanes to their next stopping place. He pulled up and switched off the engine.

'Ready?'

His eyes lingered on her a little too long and she had to turn away.

'Ready,' she muttered, her fixed firmly on the road ahead.

'Darcie, I wish you'd — ' He hesitated, clearly uncertain.

'Don't,' she said, twisting and turning her hands in her lap as she spoke. 'Please. Glenn. This is difficult enough for me — being here with you. Don't make it any worse. It's going to be a long enough night as it is.'

'I see,' he said tightly. 'You really hate me that much?'

She didn't reply, but stepped out of the Land-Rover and started off towards the footpath. She strolled out into the moonlight, not expecting to see anything untoward and almost fell backwards when she saw two dark shapes mounting the fences surrounding a field.

'Glenn!' she hissed. 'Glenn, I think it's them!'

He came over to her, his eyes searching the field until he saw them, two dark sinister shapes.

'Darcie, get back into the car. The radio's set up for a direct link with the sergeant. Tell him our exact location. We're going to nail these lowlife!'

'What about you?' She put out her hand as he made to walk away. 'Where are you going?'

'I'm going to stop them before they do any more damage!'

'Be careful, Glenn,' she said urgently.

He looked back at her and laughed a low, mocking laugh.

'Do you really care?' he whispered and then he was gone, crouching low, keeping to the cover of the bushes as he skirted the field.

Did she care? Of course she did. If he only knew it, she loved him and would have gone on loving him for the rest of her life if he hadn't deceived her so cruelly.

Darcie ran back to the car and made the call to Sergeant Greaves.

'Where's Glenn?' the sergeant asked her.

'He's gone after them,' she said and then heard Sergeant Greaves' angry exhalation at the other end.

'What's on earth is he playing at?' he snapped. 'I thought I made it clear to everyone concerned that there were to be no heroics! Look, keep low, Darcie. I don't want you putting yourself in danger, too. I'll be there in five minutes with back-up.'

10

There were three horses in the field, standing on the far side where a bramble hedge separated them from a field of sheep.

The two men were moving in on the horses in a pincer movement. Darcie felt a thrill of fear. Where was Glenn?

Clutching the torch in her hand, she hoped, when she turned it on, it would be enough to scare them away. But first, she had to get close enough.

The horses, used to people and to being handled, only shifted slightly at the approach of the man. They were such trusting, inoffensive creatures.

Darcie broke into a run. Where on earth was Glenn? Why didn't he do something?

She scrambled over the fence and charged across the open field. The men were getting closer to the horses all the time. Then, just as she thought they were about to strike, another dark shape appeared from the cover of the bushes.

The horses, properly startled now, reared and ran, putting as much distance between themselves and the men as possible. There was shouting, cursing . . .

Darcie flicked on the torch and fixed the men in the powerful beam, three of them, struggling. She saw the savage silver glint of a blade seconds before one of the men fell. Darcie shouted a warning as the two men crouched over the crumpled form on the ground.

They looked up, saw her coming towards them and rushed back the way they'd come, leaving the third figure lying helpless on the ground.

'Glenn!' she screamed. If anything happened to him, she couldn't bear it. Loving him was bad enough, losing him would destroy her! He was lying on his side, perfectly still. She fell to her knees and cautiously reached out.

'Glenn . . . Oh, Glenn, darling, are you all right?'

He rolled over on to his back and groaned softly.

'Darling?' he whispered, his voice racked with pain. 'Am I hearing things?'

He managed a mocking smile which she tried very hard to ignore. How could he lie there in pain and still tease her?

'How badly are you hurt?'

'Just a scratch,' he breathed. 'Did you get through to Sergeant Greaves?'

'Yes, I did. Don't talk, Glenn.'

She shone the torch over his body and saw the sleeve of his jacket was dark red, the fabric torn. Working quickly, she took the bandage she always carried in the pocket of her jacket and bound the wound. Normally she used it to fashion an emergency muzzle!

It was difficult working in the darkness, having to keep checking with the torch that she was actually treating the right place.

'Listen, Darcie . . . ' His voice was

alarmingly weak. She pressed her fingers against his neck. His pulse was sluggish.

'Don't talk,' she instructed again, her voice firm although inside she was frightened to death.

Then she saw the other wound in his chest. How could she have missed it? Swiftly, she pushed her hand inside his clothing and applied gentle pressure to the wound, praying that help wouldn't be too much longer arriving. She almost wept with relief when she heard the wail of sirens.

'They're here, Glenn,' she said. 'You're going to be all right.'

A smile flickered across his dear face and she bent down to kiss his cheek.

'Hold on, darling, please,' she begged.

'Why?' She thought he was teasing, but his tone was deadly serious. 'Why do you want me to hang on, Darcie?'

'Because I love you,' she blurted. 'You awful, horrid man! I love you.'

★ ★ ★

Darcie sat alone in the hospital waiting-room. A kind nurse had brought her a cup of tea, but she was still waiting desperately for news. When she heard someone entering the room, she swung round, but it was only Sergeant Greaves.

'Any news?'

'Not yet.' She tried a brave smile, but it nearly resulted in her bursting into tears.

'We caught them,' he said. 'They're not known criminals, but we've been able to match their fingerprints to those found in a number of robberies.'

He reached out and rested his hand on her shoulder.

'I need to speak to Glenn as soon as he's conscious.'

A doctor now came in and Darcie got slowly to her feet.

'Good news, Miss Westbrook,' he said. 'Mr Hunter lost a lot of blood and he's very weak, but — '

'Can I see him?'

'Of course — Sergeant?'

Sergeant Greaves smiled. 'Go ahead. I can wait.'

It was all she could do to restrain herself from running ahead of the doctor and through the doors where she knew Glenn would be waiting. He'd been moved into a side ward and was reclining, eyes closed, against several pillows. A nurse, standing beside the bed, adjusted the drip, then looked up at Darcie and smiled before hurrying away.

She stopped, several feet from the bed, suddenly overwhelmed with love for him. She thought her heart would stop beating.

Perhaps I should go, she thought. Get away from here and out of his life, go to Australia and forget all about Glenn Hunter. Perhaps it would be the kindest thing I could do for both of us. She'd seen for herself that he was alive and recovering and that was all she needed to know. Slowly, she turned away but hadn't gone two steps when she heard his voice.

'Don't you dare!'

She swung round. His eyes were open and looking at her, holding her still in the power of his gaze.

'Come here.'

'No, I — '

'Damn it, Darcie! I can't get out of bed and chase you so do as you're told for once in your life.'

Trembling, she walked towards him, towards his outstretched hand and his loving eyes. Her hand, almost of its own volition, went out to meet his and was clasped in a surprisingly strong grip.

'That's a good girl,' he murmured. 'Now, kiss me.'

'Glenn, I . . . '

'Would you refuse a sick man his dying wish?'

'Don't say that!' she cried, reliving all the fear and dread she'd felt when she thought she'd lost him.

'Why? Why not, Darcie?'

'Because . . . ' She hesitated. She couldn't say it, she just couldn't.

'Say it, Darcie — say it again! I was

barely conscious last time and I'm not sure whether I was simply dreaming.'

His voice was so gentle, so compassionate and yet so demanding. She closed her eyes and at once, his thumb began to make tiny circles in the palm of her hand, stirring her to greater feelings.

When she dared to open her eyes again, he was still looking at her. She couldn't deny it a moment longer. If she didn't say it, then surely she'd burst!

'Because I love you!'

She laughed out loud. There, she'd said it, and how wonderful it felt to admit it, to see the loving, relieved look on Glenn's face, and to know he had been waiting just as long to hear the words as she had to say them.

He lifted her hand to his lips and kissed each finger in turn, sending electrifying jolts straight to her heart, while all the time, his eyes met with hers as if they shared their very souls.

'I love you, too,' he whispered. 'And

when I get out of here, I'm going to show you just how much!'

'You talk too much,' she said, and, leaning over the bed, she kissed him, a long, lingering kiss that promised so much more.

'Hey,' he said when she finally drew away. 'I'm not supposed to get excited!'

'I'll give you excitement,' she said, pretending to be cross and wagging her finger at him.

'I was hoping you'd say that,' he said, his sparkling eyes suddenly sombre again. 'I meant what I said, Darcie. I love you. I'll never do anything to hurt you . . . '

His eyes were growing heavy. He was fighting to stay awake.

'Rest now, darling,' she whispered, kissing his forehead and tucking his hand back beneath the sheets. 'I'll be back tomorrow and the next day and every day for ever after.'

She took a final long, lingering look at him sleeping peacefully, before leaving the hospital.

There was still the spectre of Eighty Acres. She tried to push it from her mind, but it remained there, stubbornly refusing to allow her to snatch her chance of happiness. Perhaps all that had been said was simply in the heat of the moment . . .

She went home to bed, but couldn't sleep. All night, thoughts of Glenn invaded her dreams and more than once, she was brought out of a dream, woken by her own voice calling his name.

★   ★   ★

The following day, Darcie went to the hospital, armed with flowers and chocolates, fully expecting to find Glenn lying in bed. But he wasn't there and when she looked up, it was to find him sitting by the window, looking out at the windswept grounds of the cottage hospital, miles away in a world of his own.

'Glenn . . . '

He turned around to face her and his eyes positively lit up at the welcome sight of her lovely face. Her heart did a somersault, and she fought to remain outwardly cool as she sat down beside him.

'You look a lot better than you did last night,' she said awkwardly, wondering how much of the night before he could remember.

'I feel a lot better.' He grinned. 'I'm glad you're here, Darcie. I want to talk to you about Eighty Acres.' There was a note of urgency in his voice.

She closed her eyes and shook her head. She was beginning to wish she'd never set her sights on that piece of land! It had caused her nothing but trouble and heartache.

'No — ' she began.

'I'm going to talk and you're going to damn well listen for once in your life,' he said, the effort of speaking clearly tiring him.

'Not now — '

'Yes, now. I've put this off long

enough as it is. Listen to me, Darcie. Before I bought Eighty Acres, I'd already agreed with Lord Horrington exactly what we were going to do with it. The riding centre for the disabled, you know about. As for the rest — we're setting up the Horrington Trust, a charitable organisation which we had every intention of handing over to you.'

She'd been trying not to listen, to block out his words, but they were getting through and she could hardly make sense of what she was hearing.

'I don't understand.' Tears clouded her eyes.

'Can't you see it yet?' he whispered. 'We're giving you the bulk of the land to extend your sanctuary.'

Could this be true? If it was, then she'd done him a terrible injustice by never giving him the chance to explain his part in the purchase of Eighty Acres. She'd thought the worst of him without hearing his side of things and had been only too willing to accept that his love was a pretence.

He grasped her hand, held it within the gentle warmth of his own, his eyes searching hers.

'Well?' he whispered.

'I don't know what to say,' she murmured, now absolutely covered in confusion. 'I just . . . '

He laughed softly, his warm laughter like balm to her troubled spirit. 'Don't say anything, my love, just kiss me! I expect obedience from my future wife!'

'You're joking,' she gasped.

'Only about the obedience,' he replied, his eyes now achingly sincere. 'Not about you being my wife! I've loved you from the very first moment I saw you, Darcie.'

With laughter in her heart, she leaned forward into his gentle embrace and kissed him. From the power of his response, she knew it wouldn't be very long before he was back on his feet. He threaded his fingers through her soft hair.

'Just you wait,' he said. 'We've a lot of

catching up to do.'

'Oh, I'll wait.' Darcie laughed, nestling against him. She'd wait for ever if she had to, but somehow she knew it just wasn't going to take that long.

★ ★ ★

It was a fine, bright day outside, crisp and frosty, but inside the Register Office it was warm.

Darcie slid her hand into Glenn's and he gave hers a squeeze, love shining in his eyes for his beautiful, new wife.

'I think it's traditional to kiss the bride!' Lord Horrington whispered.

'Well, we can't be doing away with tradition, can we?' Glenn chuckled and drew Darcie into his arms for a long, slow kiss.

'No regrets?' he asked as they finally drew apart.

'No regrets,' she replied, eyes sparkling with happiness.

This was nothing like that other wedding with all its pomp and ceremony.

This was simplicity, but it meant so much more. This was real.

Just Darcie and Glenn and a small handful of close friends. She wouldn't have wanted a big white wedding in the little village church. This had to be their day, hers and Glenn's, and bear no painful reminders of the past.

Lord Horrington pushed open the door and they stepped outside into the bright winter sunshine. Snow had fallen while they were inside and everywhere was covered in a glistening mantle of white.

At first, Darcie wondered who all the people were. She looked around, held her breath . . .

There was Betty and Mandy . . . and the Strawson family . . . a small crowd of students from the college . . .

She looked around. She recognised them all, although didn't know all their names. Her heart soared. They'd come all this way to town to wish her and Glenn well . . .

Darcie thought of the two tables they

had booked in a local restaurant for the wedding breakfast and her heart nose-dived. How she wished they could all come, too, all these people who cared so much.

Her eyes clouded and a small frown wrinkled her forehead.

'I took the liberty of cancelling your tables,' Lord Horrington said, somewhat bashfully. 'When I realised all these people were planning to turn up, I hired coaches for them and — and, well, I've invited them all back to Horrington Hall for dinner. You, too — as guests of honour! I hope that was all right. I know you both wanted a quiet wedding.'

'Oh, thank you!' Darcie cried, flinging her arms round his neck and planting a grateful kiss on his cheek. Then she turned to look around.

'Thank you all.'

She felt Glenn's arm wind round her waist and pull her close.

This was the happiest day of her life and the tears that frosted on her cheeks were tears of happiness.

'I think they'd like an encore of the after-wedding kiss,' Lord Horrington whispered.

Once again, Glenn and Darcie obliged and this time it was to a chorus of cheers and applause.

THE END

Other titles in the
Linford Romance Library:

WILD FOR LOVE

Carol MacLean

Polly is an ecologist, passionate and uncompromising about wildlife rights. Against all her principles she falls in love with Jake, heir to a London media empire, whose development company is about to destroy a beautiful marsh. But can love ever blossom between two such different people? As Polly battles to save the marsh and learns to compromise for love, Jake finally finds the life he has always desired . . .

FREE FALL

Phyllis Humphrey

Jennifer Gray, working with Colin Thomas on a sports promotion, doesn't like her job. He's a pilot, skydiver and owner of Skyway Aviation — and she's afraid of heights! Despite feelings of jealousy over Colin's love interest, he's not the man for her. However, Colin, knows a good thing when he sees it. So will his humour, sensitivity and old-fashioned charm help Jennifer overcome her fear of heights and convince her their relationship is just what she needs?

LOVE OR MARRIAGE

Fay Cunningham

When Hope rubs an old teapot, the last thing she expects is for a genie to appear. But Finn Masters is very real — and very attractive. Finn's financial problems and the old house he has inherited are none of Hope's business. She is already engaged to Todd and plans for the wedding are underway, so falling in love with Finn is not a good idea. Luckily, she still has one of her three wishes left.